Suo sibi gladio hunc jugulo.

I will cut this man's throat with his own sword.

—Terence, *The Brothers,* V, viii, 35

In this war there are no rules, there is no referee. I am the ally, and I am the enemy. And only I will decide the weapons and the arena.

—Mack Bolan, THE EXECUTIONER

The bestselling adventure series in the country!

THE EXECUTIONER

And more to come . . .

THE EXECUTIONER:

Jersey Guns

by
Don Pendleton

PINNACLE BOOKS • NEW YORK CITY

THE EXECUTIONER: JERSEY GUNS

An original Pinnacle Books edition, published for the
first time anywhere.

ISBN: 0-523-00328-5

First printing, January 1974

Printed in the United States of America

PINNACLE BOOKS, INC.
275 Madison Avenue
New York, N.Y. 10016

Dedicated with pride and congratulations to the edge-of-hell guys of Vietnam—both those who returned and those who never will—of whom it is now being said, "Your war is over." For now, sure, let's hope so. Bolan's is not. Nor, in the deeper truth, will yours ever be.

PROLOGUE

Mack Bolan's most persistent nightmare usually found him waist-deep in a flowing river of blood, sticky undercurrents swirling between his legs and trying to pull him down into the flow which also bore faceless mangled bodies with great gaping wounds. The river groaned as it flowed, alive with the muted symphony of violent dying by the legion who had tasted Bolan's simple applications of criminal justice.

It was a narrow river.

On the one bank were amassed the forces of law and order, grim and silent men who stood in disciplined ranks and fired volleys at his head to the cadenced commands of none other than the President of the United States.

On the opposite bank was a yowling mob of enraged *mafiosi*. These were scampering about their side of the river in a disorganized and sometimes hysterical fashion, dashing this way and that in a cacophony of gunfire and obscene shoutings, throwing at him everything within their reach, including stones and bones, in addition to the whistling spray of bullets. Now and then a triumphantly screaming band of these would rush down from the high ground overlooking the river, bearing above their heads something almost human, which they gleefully lofted at him from the bank; Bolan inevitably caught the grisly object in outflung arms . . . and it was always the same *sort* of thing—a "turkey"—a thing which had once been a sentient human form but was now reduced to a blob of mindless flesh—mutilated and shredded by a fiendish method of torture that ensured the victim a slow and agonizing death.

Bolan always awakened at this point. Not even in the subconscious realm could he confront "turkey meat" without a mind-wrenching reaction.

And, of course, in the deeper sense, Bolan's recurring dream was not a nightmare at all. A nightmare usually portrays some dreaded but unlikely situation—a frightening experience from which the dreamer may awaken to a much more comfortable reality.

There was no comfortable reality to which Bolan may awaken.

The "nightmare" was merely a replay in symbology of the man's normal, workaday world.

Mack Bolan was the "Executioner."

He'd been accorded the chilling tag while serving as a soldier in his country's service . . . during another nightmare called Vietnam. As a member of the most modern army in the world, Bolan had been finely trained in the oldest of the arts of warfare—*killing*—and he had become most proficient in his assigned specialty.

He was perhaps the only American soldier in the Southeast Asian theater to carry an enemy price tag on his head. As leader of an elite penetration team, Bolan had ranged throughout enemy-held territories on "kill missions" directed against specific targets. The "Executioner" tag accorded him was meant as a tribute to his effectiveness—a tribute by a grateful government and by his peers in the field.

When the Executioner returned to home soil to

wage the same brand of unrelenting warfare against a different enemy, however, he knew that he could expect no plaudits from either his government or his society. A declared War Against the Mafia, on Bolan's terms, could bring nothing but official denunciation and forceful reaction.

> The law can't stop the mob . . . can't even touch them. Someone has to. I guess what is needed here is a war against the cannibals. The same kind of war we fought in 'Nam. Sure, it's going to be a lonely battle. But so were all the others. And this one I *know* I can't win. So who said you have to win 'em all? Sometimes the most important thing is to simply *fight* them all. This is one I have to fight.

So saying, Bolan began his one-man response to the menace of syndicated crime, the illegal combine which had been characterized by official spokesmen as "the nation's invisible second government."

Bolan *knew* . . . the Mafia *did* exist—it was the most insistent and insidious threat ever faced by men of noble intentions anywhere, and he felt most strongly the obligation to oppose this spreading cancer which was threatening to destroy the institutions of American life.

The story that follows is the seventeenth installment of Bolan's war chronicle. Still alive and fighting his way along the "last bloody mile" of his hell on earth, the Executioner has just left behind him a monumental slaughter in Sicily, the home and training ground of the Mafia.

Wounded and soul-weary, Bolan is on his way back to the U.S. San Diego and Philadelphia are still repairing the damage of Bolan's most recent hits. Never before had the Mafia been hit with such quick devastation.

A short rest in Algiers hadn't really been enough to prepare Bolan for any immediate action. He knew that they'd be looking for him at every gateway city in the U.S. He also knew that they'd expect him to hit where the action was—wherever the law seemed to be overwhelmed by the underworld.

Boston and Washington were fairly quiet; the local Mafia chapters were still licking their wounds and attempting to put themselves back together.

Things were pretty lively in the Seattle area, though, surprisingly so. And Detroit showed signs of needing some attention. Maybe later . . .

But it was Bolan's thought to follow-up on his Philly job . . . and trace some of the missing links to the Manhattan strongholds. And between Philly and New York stood the Garden State of New Jersey.

A scattering of bedroom communities in Jersey served the Philly-New York axis, and within twenty miles of Times Square, there were at least sixty homes of top *Mafiosi*—quiet, well-manicured ranch-styles and split-levels. The big action and the bloody deals were kept out of these tree-lined communities. Everything should be nice and peaceful in the neighborhood, right? Gotta maintain the respectable image. No crab-grass, no hippies . . . and no fuzz, either.

So, though much of suburban Jersey was quiet and practically devoid of crime statistics, the land was virtually crawling with *Mafiosi*. Mack Bolan thought it might be interesting to visit the boys at home, to see what the big Jersey guns are up to, and how their garden grows . . .

1 DEATH STALK

It was easier getting back into Jersey than it was getting out. That mad flight out of Teterboro was only a month ago, though it seemed like a year. Some itinerary—Jersey to Sicily, Sicily to Algiers, Algiers to Jersey. Who'd believe it?

Someone did, evidently, someone who knew it wasn't going to be Seattle or Detroit. And now Death was tailgating him across that moonwashed Jersey countryside—Death with a capital *D* but spelled *Taliferi*—and it was crowding the rearview mirror of his Mustang with blinding headlights and awaiting only the most efficient place to happen.

Bolan had identified the big crew wagon the moment it swung in behind him; he knew who they were and how they would try it. The *Taliferi* knew the death game quite well. It was their profession, their calling, their primary function in life.

The Talifero brothers, Pat and Mike, were the lord high enforcers of the national combine. They took orders from only *la Commissione,* and their hit crews constituted a standing army of elite storm troopers such as had not been seen this side of Hitler's Germany. No "button men," these—no bumbling hit men or muscle specialists—these guys were Gestapo and, yeah, they knew their business.

Mack Bolan, thankfully, also knew his.

His business was to stay alive, to carry the war back to the Bloody Brotherhood, and to walk up their backs every chance he could find.

Forever the realist, however, Bolan knew that his business, at this moment, was at the verge of bankruptcy.

He was carrying an agonizing souvenir of his Sicilian encounter his in his ribs and in a painful and stubbornly seeping flesh wound of the lower leg. He was bruised and scratched and hurting like hell from head to toe . . . and he was weary enough to simply let go and die.

State troopers were swarming the New Jersey Turnpike and busily sealing every exit along that hundred-mile corridor between Philly and New York. Through some inexplicable extension of the combat sense—or of survival instincts—Bolan had sniffed out that maneuver and made his escape from the toll road at almost the last possible moment.

And now here he was, cruising a lonely back road across central New Jersey with a Talifero head party at his rear bumper.

The sanest thing for a guy in this situation would be to simply let go and let it happen. It would be so easy, so quick, so final.

He'd been a dead man since this damn war began, anyway.

Yeah.

Make it official, Bolan. Stop and die for the men.

He had been cruising at an inconspicuous sixty miles an hour since leaving the turnpike, and when the Talifero meat wagon slid up behind him, he'd watched them nuzzle up and look him over, then drop back again for a pacing into a likely shooting gallery.

The road was narrow and curvy, picking its way through the jumble of factories, farms, and small towns to the east of Trenton. At this hour of the night, only death was stirring along its winding route.

Just the same, the death crew would be looking for optimum conditions; these boys hardly ever left anything to chance; they were not gamblers, they were sure-thingers.

Bolan sighed as he casually checked the clip in the AutoMag. Three rounds of .44-caliber massive death were all that remained for the big silver pistol. The Beretta was totally defanged, empty, useless.

Sure. Time to stop and die, Bolan.

He angled a faint smile into the rearview mirror and quietly declared, "The hell you say."

His foot came down hard on the accelerator, and the rented Mustang leaped forward in instant response, leaving a puff of exhaust gases to mark the spot where the "death stalk" became a two-sided game.

The big Cadillac surged forward also, under expert command and grimly hanging into the tail slot. The Mustang, though, had been designed for games of this nature. The early advantage was clearly hers. The sleek sportsters swept over the abrupt ridges and power-screamed through the sharp curves as though all the laws of motion had been written into her design specifications—and slowly but surely a gap began forming between the speeding vehicles.

Bolan was playing only for numbers, though, not miles—counting the seconds of lead he managed to hold into each turn, calculating the increase with each successive maneuver and pitching his combat mind forward into that moment of confrontation which lay inevitably somewhere on the road ahead.

He knew that one crew wagon on his tail also inexorably meant that others were streaking into the chase—from several directions, no doubt. The fact that they had picked up on him so quickly was no matter of chance or accident. These boys were radio-equipped and -dispatched. They were as good as the cops in an exercise like this one; and in this particular case they had an advantage over the cops—they knew the car Bolan was driving.

Damn right, these guys knew their business. They had to. It was their only excuse for living. And Bolan had been making monkeys of them for much too long. They meant to get him this time, obviously, and that meat patrol that was now about ten seconds off his rear bumper represented but one statement in that determination.

So, sure . . . it had to be a game of numbers. He could not simply outrun them. He had to stop them cold, and he had to do it before the others had time to join the chase.

And so it was when the Mustang screamed into a darkened crossroads with the Taliferi less than fifteen seconds behind. Bolan caught a brief glimpse of a road sign just as he powered into the intersection; one way led to the town of Roosevelt, the other to Perrineville. Neither meant a thing to Bolan. He was seeking *terrain,* not towns—a place with combat stretch—and his instincts swung him eastward, toward Perrineville.

And he found his combat stretch several minutes and twenty numbers later, at a point where the road topped a gentle rise to descend abruptly into a double switch back and over a narrow brook.

He nearly missed the bridge, himself, the Mustang toeing in at the last possible instant to flash across, a hair width removed from the concrete abutment. Then it took him another ten or twelve precious numbers to halt that forward plunge and to bring the Mustang around in a whining return. He killed the lights and swung her broadside across the narrow bridge, then hobbled up the hillside—sternly commanding his injured leg to behave itself.

The glow of swiftly advancing headlights was peeking over the hill as he took up his position. Then the chase car was into the switchback, burning rubber in the sudden slow-down, rocking with the momentum of the double curve at high speed, and struggling for a path onto the bridge.

He could see them clearly as they groaned past his position, could feel the alarm and consternation as eight sets of shoulders hunched forward into the do-or-die curve.

The windows were down. Bolan could hear the cry of warning that erupted from the rear seat as the headlights swept onto that abandoned vehicle at bridge-center.

His own leg kicked in reflex as another panicky leg straightened on the brake pedal and that big limousine with eight headhunters aboard went into its death slide.

The Caddy was out of control even as it reached

the bridge, hunching down onto locked wheels and crabbing into the narrow passageway.

The rear end struck the approach abutment a glancing blow, slamming the heavy vehicle into a full fishtail and a broadside plunge along the bridge —twenty-one feet of Detroit steel grindingly attempting to fit itself within a fifteen-foot cement straitjacket.

The crew wagon was a disaster of disintegrating metal even before it reached the Mustang. It blew on, taking the smaller car with it to the other side. Bolan's vehicle fell away there and spun off onto the embankment, flipped, and came to rest on its top in the brook. The other car took an end-over-end tumble off the roadway and rolled on for another thirty feet or so before shuddering to a final halt on its side.

Bolan began his approach in a complete and deathly silence. A moment later came the weak cries and ghastly mouthings that assured him that he was not getting off all that easy—a mop-up operation was clearly in order.

One of the hardmen had been ejected from the vehicle during that wild plunge across the bridge. The remains were obviously beyond mop-up and even beyond identification; it looked as though he'd been caught in that meat grinder between rending metal and abrasive cement.

Bolan stepped around the soggy pile of hamburger and went on across the bridge, moving slowly to favor the protesting leg and warily approaching the pile of junk which had seconds earlier been a proud testament to man's engineering excellence.

He encountered another grisly bag of pulverized

flesh on the roadway at the point where the crew wagon had taken off on its cross-country roll. From that point he had only to follow the trail of broken bodies, counting three more between the road and the shattered vehicle.

That would leave three still to be accounted for; and from the sounds of the night, they would soon be beyond mop-up also.

The vehicle was lying in the shadows of high bushes, but with enough illumination from the bright moonlight for Bolan to see the two men who were folded into that steel trap.

And, yeah, they were in bad shape.

Both were conscious, though, and carrying on a groaning conversation.

"Can't feel my legs. Think my back's broke."

"How 'bout Carlo? Where's Carlo?"

"Fuck Carlo. Where's that fuckin' *guy?* Where's *he?*"

"Dunno. Who cares now? We're gonna die here, Bill."

"Maybe *you* are."

"We both are."

Bolan joined the conversation then, his voice low-pitched and coated with ice.

"Yeah, you both are," he announced solemnly.

A hand moved into the wreckage to pluck a revolver from numbed fingers. Another hand came in and clamped itself over a bloodied mouth and nose.

"How many in there?" asked the ice man.

The one who had been addressed as Bill replied, "That you, Bolan?"

"It's me."

11

"I knew we'd meet someday."

"Congratulations, you were right."

Bill groaned and gargled deep in his throat as he asked, "What're you doing?"

"Mopping up."

"Leave us be."

"Can't."

The guy moaned and tried unsuccessfully to move his head for a better look at the big cold bastard outside. "What're you doing to Campy?"

"Helping him die."

"Bastard!"

"Don't feel left out," the cold voice suggested, and the hand moved to the other face.

"Wait! Goddamn it, wait a minute!"

"Too long already."

The guy was mumbling angrily into Bolan's fingers. "Look, don't! Lemme die my own way!"

Bolan slid the hand aside. "Okay," he said quietly. "If you want to die talking."

"About what?"

"How many crews are after me?"

The guy snickered, choked, coughed painfully, then told the big man outside, "Enough. You're dead already, bud."

"So give me something to worry about."

"You'll never get out of this fuckin' state alive."

"How many crews, Matthew?"

The guy coughed again, and sticky warmth flowed onto Bolan's fingers. He turned the head to keep the guy from choking on his own blood, and again asked, "How many?"

"Fuck ya. Die wondering."

Bolan replied, "Okay," and went away from there.

The piercing odor of gasoline vapors was strong in his senses as he stepped around the rear of the wreckage; and then a movement in the bushes a few yards away sent him in a sprawling dive toward the shadows.

He had a flashing perception of a large bulk of a man with a pistol outstretched and spitting flame at him; in that same instant the entire area was brilliantly illuminated by flames as the gasoline vapors ignited with a whooshing explosion.

He felt the bullet from that fateful firing sing past him. By the time he had completed his roll and was coming up to return the fire, his target was a staggering fireball, the brightest thing of the night, spinning in confusion and seeking an escape from the inescapable.

The guy must have been lying in gasoline, soaked in it.

Bolan's appropriated revolver instinctively jerked into the firing lineup and pumped three quick mercy rounds into that tortured hell on earth . . . and he walked quickly away without looking back.

Afoot now, bleeding anew from the old wounds, and with a thousand Jersey guns awaiting him somewhere out there, Bolan nevertheless sent out a quiet "thanks" to the universe at large.

For the moment, at least, he was leaving death behind him.

2 THE FARM

He dreamed interminably of the infinite river and eternal warfare, and he awoke somewhere within that eternity with bright sunlight upon his face.

He was lying in straw, and he was naked. The sunlight was coming through an overhead window, a sort of skylight set into a high ceiling. He was warm, woozy, completely without pain.

A large man in blue jeans and a striped shirt sat on a bench beside him, watching him with attentive eyes.

Someone else was at his other side. He was too comfortable to make the effort of turning his head to see who was there.

From somewhere off in that direction came a gasp and an excited female voice. "Bruno! He's awake!"

Okay. That other someone was a woman, obviously. The big dude in blue jeans must be Bruno. So what?

Bruno looked okay. Balding, a bit overweight, pleasant face, worried eyes.

Bolan tried to ask, "Bruno *who?*" but his tongue clung to the roof of his mouth, and somehow he couldn't get it loose.

Then the woman leaned over him; and she wasn't

a woman, at all. A girl, a mere slip of a girl, dressed also in blue jeans and a shirt made from the same material as Bruno's.

Bruno's daughter?

The eyes were huge pools of dark compassion, framed in smooth flesh of almost dusky hue, but alive and glistening. Long, shiny hair fell in smooth cascades across the shoulders—jet-black, silken.

A kid, and here lay Bolan mother naked.

He made the effort and got a hand in motion, sending it to a flopping and heavy rest somewhere about the thighs. A towel was draped across him down there—or something with a terrycloth feeling.

Okay. Okay, kid, nothing to worry about, don't look so scared.

She was asking him, in a concerned but musical voice, "How do you feel?"

He tried the tongue again and gave it up, settling for a crooked smile that somehow felt all contorted and clownish.

What the hell was wrong with him?

As though reading his thoughts, the girl told him, "Bruno found you in the brook. We've stopped your bleeding, and we've given you something to ease the pain. Can you tell me how you feel?"

Reality crashed in on him, then. Somehow he got an elbow under him and tried to push himself upright. The girl pressed him back down, gently but firmly, and she told him. "You must lie still."

The tongue came unstuck, but his voice sounded like quacking as he mumbled, "No, you don't know. Danger, dangerous for you here."

She was trying to calm him, and the guy came over to place a heavy hand on his head.

He was trying to tell them that their lives were not worth a piece of the straw he was lying upon—not as long as he lay there—but he felt that he was speaking into a well, a deep well which began enlarging and closing in around him; and it was the last lucid moment he had that day.

When next he found an edge of reality he could hang on to, he was lying between soft sheets, and he felt as though he'd been dropped from a high-flying aircraft without a parachute.

The girl was seated at a window just across the room, bright sunlight streaming in on her, writing something on a large tablet which she held on her knees.

She was beautiful.

He watched her for a long moment; then her eyes raised to his with a start, and he was again impressed with the dimensions of those deep pools.

The well, maybe, into which he had become absorbed the last time around?

Bolan did not know, offhand, what else to say, so he asked her, "How long have I been here?"

"This is the second day," she replied in a voice with very little air pushing it.

"Where is it?"

"What?"

"Where am I?"

"This is . . . my bedroom. Our farm, my brother and I. Chicken ranch. Near Manalapan."

"What is Manalapan?"

"A town. On Route Thirty-three, mid-state."

"Now close to Perrineville?"

"Not far. Less than ten miles. We're just about halfway between Philadelphia and New York City."

Bolan groaned at that and raised himself to a sitting position. "Then you must have a special angel," he told the girl. "That's not nearly far enough." He swung one foot to the floor and felt himself toppling off-balance toward the headboard of the bed.

He wasn't even aware that she'd left her chair, but the girl was there instantly, arms about his shoulders, guiding him down to the proper spot on the pillows.

"Don't try that again," she commanded almost angrily. "You're not *that* tough, Mr. Bolan."

His eyes must have asked the question. She perched there beside him and answered it in a nononsense tone. "Yes, we know all about you. There's been nothing else on radio and television for the past two days. Bruno took the bullet out of your side, and we did what we could for your other hurts. The rest is up to you, though. You must lie still, or you'll bust loose and start bleeding again. How about some food? Think you could handle some?"

He muttered, "I'll eat a cow if it'll get me out of here."

"That's thanks for you," she said in a solemn little voice.

"The thanks you have coming, kid, will be a bullet up the nose if they find me here. You just can't know—"

"If you mean those hoods, they've already been here twice. We had you hidden in the brooder house all through last night."

"They'll be back," he argued. "Those guys don't know the meaning of quit. Now, you go get my clothes while I get the cobwebs out of my brain."

The girl ran from the room, and he heard her outside a moment later, calling for her brother.

Bolan made another try for the floor, and reached it, then sat there on the edge of the bed and examined himself.

The guy had done a good job with the chest wound. Very little soreness, obviously no infection. Nylon thread for stitches. He grinned wryly and pulled the injured leg up for a look-see.

Inflamed, yeah, swollen . . . and hurting like hell. The ten-mile stroll through that creek bed had not helped it at all. Some sort of evil-smelling poultice was taped over the wound. Bolan removed it and bent down for a closer look. He just hoped that Bruno had cleaned it out thoroughly before he sewed it up. He was still inspecting the mess when Bruno himself came huffing into the house.

The guy was not as old as he looked, Bolan was betting.

Looked fifty.

If he was the kid's brother, though, then he was probably somewhere under forty—certainly no more than that.

He was standing there in the doorway and filling it, a real ox of a man, giving Bolan the concerned gaze.

Bolan showed the guy a scowl and told him, "You're a good medic, Bruno. Thanks. Will you get me my pants?"

"You don't recognize me, do you?" Bruno asked quietly.

Bolan looked him over more closely, then replied, "Should I?"

18

"I guess not," the guy said. "We met only once, and you were in quite a hurry that time, too."

Bolan was giving him a quizzical smile.

"Dien Huc," the guy explained. "The field hospital. I was on duty there the time you brought that column of kids in. You know, those kids from—"

"Small world, Bruno," Bolan said tautly. "That was Doc Brantzen's headquarters."

"Right. I was one of his medics, surgical assistant."

"And now you're raising chickens."

"Right, now I'm raising chickens."

"Brantzen's dead. I got 'im killed. I'll get you killed, too, Bruno. You and that beautiful kid, both of you. Now, get me my pants and point me toward the coast."

"No way," the guy told him. "You'd never make it. Not on that leg. You could lose it yet."

"Just how bad is it?"

"Bad enough. No vital tissues lost. Everything will rebuild if you'll give it a decent chance. And if you don't lose it to infection. I've got you on antibiotics." The big guy grinned. "Same stuff I give my chickens. If you don't start crowing, I guess you'll survive it."

Bolan said, "The leg. What about it?"

"Use it too soon, and you'll lose it. Give it a couple days, anyway."

"You know I can't," Bolan growled. "The headhunters, Bruno. You know what those guys are. They won't stop with mine. They'll take yours and the kid's, just to keep in practice."

The girl stepped through the doorway and said,

"Stop calling me 'the kid.' The name is Sara, no *h*. And I'm no kid."

"That's right, she's not," Bruno told Bolan in a matter-of-fact tone. "She lost her man in 'Nam. She's a widow already."

Bolan was reminded that hot wars make many young widows, but this was ridiculous. He'd pegged her age at about sixteen.

She caught his look, and repeated, "I am *no* kid. And we didn't pull you out of the brook to make an amputee out of you. So get back in that bed and stop acting silly."

Bolan glared at her for a moment; then his gaze flicked to the man. "How long," he solemnly asked him, "do you think it will take the headhunters to put together a make on two ex-GI's—one wounded and needing medical attention, the other a surgical nurse who just happens to live in the search zone?"

"I figure it may take them another couple of days," the guy replied soberly. He spread his hands and added, "Look, man. What choice do you have?"

What choice? Bolan already knew the answer to that. It was coming from his head, in spinning circles of dizziness, and from that swollen leg, on cresting waves of pain and nausea.

"Okay," he replied weakly.

He lay back down and closed his eyes, returning very quickly to flowing rivers and eternal warfare, and to a new twist in skin-crawling nightmares—a chicken ranch overnight becoming a "turkey" farm.

Yeah. It was the grand-slammer, Doc Brantzen special. Brantzen had been the first turkey on Mack Bolan's soul. But a hell of a long way from the last one.

3 THE HEALING

They were nice people, both Sara and her brother; but during the next forty-eight hours of around-the-clock nursing, feeding, and constant attention, Bolan got to know quite a bit more about his tenders than they of him—or so he thought.

Both of these people had, in effect, already retired from the problems of life—in so many ways.

Sara, as it turned out, had just a few weeks earlier quietly marked her twenty-second birthday. She still looked sixteen to Bolan, but that was just surface stuff. Down in there where she really lived, Sara Henderson was a resigned old lady in a rocking chair, quietly filling in her days the best she could until death overcame her.

She had married David Henderson, her college sweetheart, at the age of nineteen. Two weeks later David kissed her good-bye and went to war. He did not survive. And neither did Sara. She came home —to the chicken ranch—and watched her father die of cancer. The mother had been dead for some time.

Mother and Father Tassily had emigrated from Romania just in time to get in on America's big Depression. Bruno and Sara were their only offspring—their only living kin in America—and now Bruno and Sara were all that was.

Sara ran the farm on her own until big brother Bruno came home from Vietnam; and he returned a maimed man, but not in body.

Bruno had helped the field surgeons hack off too many shattered arms and legs from despairing young men. He had seen too many savageries, too much inhumanity, and far too much senseless death and suffering. He had gone to Vietnam as a conscientious objector on medical assignment. He returned a confirmed athiest in need of considerable medical attention himself.

These were the people who were laying their lives on Bolan's line. Somehow, without actually saying so, they conveyed the idea that they did not regard the event as any sort of sacrifice, but as some weird atonement for nameless sins.

Bolan appreciated what they were doing, of course. But he was appalled by the unspoken implications that he had come along merely to collect their tithes of atonement.

During one of those quiet moments with Bruno, he had told the big Romanian, "The master clock of life doesn't beat just to the *ticks*, you know. It needs the *tocks*, as well."

And he'd told Sara, in the still hours of one of those endless nights, "When I sleep, I dream. And when I dream, I think I'm more awake than at any other time. Life is like that, Sara. Paradoxical. Every hurt carries the seed of some great joy. And every great moment has but one place to go from there, and that's back down to the valley of despair. But we *live* in neither place, you know. We live in the *middle,* and we visit the other places from time to time. Try living in the extremes—either one, Sara —and you're resigning from life."

Bolan was no preacher man. He didn't even know whether or not the things he felt made sense to anyone else, but he did feel them very strongly, and he quietly got in his points with Sara and Bruno whenever he could.

To an outside observer, it may have seemed as though Mack Bolan had been "sent" to the Tassilys. As he mended, so too did they—in so many subtle ways.

By the third day, Bruno had become much more talkative, less solemn and brooding, even humorous and playful at times.

Sara had definitely become aware of Bolan as a man. She'd taken to doing things with her hair, wearing a hint of makeup, and she'd even abandoned the blue jeans in favor of a couple of bright little fashions which she'd whipped out on her sewing machine while Bolan slept.

On that third day, also, Bruno took his chicken truck off to Manhattan on an urgent errand for his star boarder. He left at daybreak, promising to return by nightfall—otherwise, "ring the bells and say a prayer for the rummy Romanian."

Bolan was not overly worried about the safety of the mission. Bruno frequently took his own birds to market. This trip into the city would appear to be routine, in case anyone was keeping watch over the comings and goings at that farm. And he was sending the guy to a trusted friend.

They had moved Bolan back to a loft in the brooder house, which now was alive with thousands of cheeping baby chicks—the move being made at Bolan's insistence. He also took along the remainders of his war armaments—the empty Beretta, the nearly empty AutoMag, and the Talifero revolver with three live chambers.

Bruno had built him a hideaway bunk in the loft above the chicks and padded it down with clean straw covered with a couple of heavy quilts. It was very comfortable. His medications were out there, as was a variety of high-protein "nibblings"—cheeses, boiled eggs, and so on. In addition to that, Sara came out every couple of hours and poked a ration of hot food into him.

On the morning which saw Bruno off to Manhattan, Sara came to the loft at eight o'clock with tape measure, pad, and pencil in hand.

"What's that for?" Bolan had growled at her.

"To see where you're at, with what," she'd replied, twinkling, and took his measurements at every conceivable point and angle.

A couple of times during that operation their eyes locked for overlong periods, and it seemed that things were getting a bit out of hand.

She'd gone out of there without another word, though, and at ten o'clock she was back, with a very close copy of his favored combat outfit—a black, skin-tight two-piecer with all the handy pockets in the right places.

Bolan was deeply impressed.

"How'd you do that?" he marveled.

"Just a little something I whipped up," the girl replied, trying to conceal her pride in the production. "It wasn't all that hard."

She handed him a folded sheet of heavy paper.

He recognized it immediately as coming from the large writing tablet which he'd seen in her possession so often. Obviously the tablet was an artist's sketchpad, and she had very artistically sketched Bolan, probably as he lay sleeping in her presence, but as she'd imagined him to look in full combat regalia. All of it was there—the weapons, the utility belts, the gadgets—and she'd captured a catlike poise in that rangy body as well as a savagely snarling face which somehow still had a somewhat saintly cast to it.

Very quietly he asked her, "Is that the way I look to you?"

"Yes," she replied, just as quietly.

"How'd you get the combat rig?" he asked.

She shrugged daintily. "Lifted it. I guess you've been sketched by every police artist in the country. I've seen it many times, in the papers."

He said, "I see."

"Try it on. The suit."

"Later," he told her, sighing.

"I've seen your pinky toes before, plenty of times."

"Later, just the same," he murmured.

"Mack Bolan, I believe you're a hopeless prude," she told him. She leaned across the bunk and pulled the sheet away from him, all the way, fastidiously folding it at his feet.

This, Bolan was thinking, was where he'd come in.

Except that now there was not even a towel to protect his sense of modesty.

This was, however, very obviously no time for modesty.

Sara was removing her dress, carefully folding it with the same studied movements with which she'd handled the bedsheet. She laid the dress atop the packing crate that Bolan was using as a night stand, then went to the window for a quick peek outside.

"Am I ready for this?" he asked her, feeling silly with the words even as they left his mouth.

"I don't know about you," she replied, turning to him with a solemn smile. "But I sure am."

"Well, hell . . ."

Sara was removing her bra as she retraced the path to Bolan's bunk. It was odd, he was thinking, how clothing made some girls look so underdeveloped when in fact they were not . . . like this one. She was beautifully put together. The breasts were on the delicate side, but perfectly formed, stiffish, and tightly packed—incredibly glossy.

She put the bra with the dress, then hooked both thumbs into the waistband of her panties and just stood there gazing at him with those limpid eyes.

She seemed frozen there, suddenly, the panties ever so slightly lowered, a statue in glowing flesh tones.

Bolan noticed, then, that those hands were trembling. He took one in his and told her, "Be sure you know what you're doing. This is very probably your last chance to back out."

"You're not helping a bit," she protested faintly in a wobbly voice. "I rehearsed and rehearsed. Had it all figured out—what I'd say, what you'd say— and you're not *doing* it."

He said, "No rehearsals needed, Sara. Not if this is what you truly want."

She cried, "Oh, God, I *do!*" And with that she

broke down completely, hiding her face in her hands and bawling her heart out.

He pulled her on down with him, and gently made room for her, and consoled her with loving touches and reassuring words, and she very quickly became fully a woman in his arms as each to their own need they found that special healing which somehow seems to justify the pains of the world.

And, some time later, Bolan admiringly told her, "You were right, Sara. You're sure no kid."

They lay in slack embrace and talked of various things for quite a while—serious things, silly things, man-woman things—and after they'd run out of words they simply clung to each other in a silent communion outside of time.

Later he donned the black suit for her pleased inspection, then left it on as they snuggled into another quiet mood.

Somewhere along toward early afternoon, Bolan fell into a deep sleep. It was probably his most peaceful rest in weeks, and he did not know when Sarah left.

He awoke with a start, alone, with the sun low in the sky and perfectly framed in his window—and with some animal comprehension of danger.

There had been an outcry from down by the house—a human cry or shout or something—coming in right at the edge of his consciousness, but weakly commanding attention.

He carried the AutoMag to the window and gazed down upon the familiar scene, normally so tranquil.

This time, though, the view sent combat hormones leaping into his bloodstream and coursing immediately to every reach of his system.

A strange vehicle was parked in the drive, near the house. Two guys in fancy silk threads were down there in open view, standing beside the car. One of them was holding a door open, and the other was trying to force a grimly struggling Sara Henderson into the vehicle.

It was one of those sudden-confrontation situations that allow for no combat brief, no tactical planning, no exercise of the intellect whatsoever. And it was sheer conditioned reflex of the combat sense that sent the AutoMag crashing through that flimsy pane of glass, that lined up those doomsday sights, that squeezed the fist that closed the switch that sent 240 grains of screaming death sizzling across that forty-yard range to the target.

The big magnum bullet tore past within inches of that lovely face he'd kissed so tenderly such a short while ago and thwacked home between two startled eyes with what Sara would later describe as "a horrible sucking sound."

Even as that first round was impacting target, the big silver hogleg was roaring another angry bellow, and missile number two was annihilating another firetrack; the dude at the car door found himself with an inexplicably exploding throat, and the two of them died hardly a gasp apart.

Sara had collapsed onto her knees. She was kneeling there in the gore surrounding her, hands clasped in her lap, looking up at him and screaming something unintelligible.

She had quieted down somewhat by the time he reached her, but she was still kneeling there between those two citations of sudden death, and her first anguished words for the Executioner were: "No, Mack, God, no, you shouldn't have! Now they've found you!"

He plucked her out of there and steered her toward the house as he replied to that.

"They have," he said icily. "The hard way."

4 THE MESSAGE

He gave her brandy and scrubbed the blood spatterings from that beloved flesh as she chatteringly related the happening for his interested ears.

The two *mafiosi* had barged in and searched the house, for the third time that week. They'd even checked the dirty laundry, counted toothbrushes in the bathroom, and pawed through the garbage cans.

The younger one had been ordered to search the outbuildings, but according to Sara, he'd done no more than stroll nervously about the grounds and peer warily through partially open doorways.

Then the big one had started pushing Sara about and trying to scare her with broad hints about the penalty "for harboring fugitives."

They'd tried to pass themselves off as "detectives."

It proved to be Sara's undoing.

She unloaded a pile of outrage upon them and finished off by denouncing them as "two-bit hoods."

Apparently it had seemed to the boys that she protested too much.

They decided to "take her downtown" for

"further questioning," and that was where Bolan entered the scene.

He was damned glad he had.

There was seldom any return from those "trips downtown" with the Taliferi.

He asked Sara, "The big guy seemed to be in charge?"

She replied, "Uh-huh."

"Was his name ever mentioned? What was he called?"

"Hugger. Yes, he called him Hugger."

Bolan showed her a thin smile and said, "Great. Now, let's get the voice. Where was it pitched? Here? Here?"

He was giving her a scale of probabilities, and she stopped him at about middle C.

"Good girl. This could be important, so let's make sure we get it right. How about tonal quality? Did he talk like this?" He'd offered her an example of a nasal sound; then he tried her with a grating foghorn: "Or more like this?"

Sara was shaking her head and watching him with growing interest, thoroughly captivated by the virtuoso performance. He finally satisfied her on the basics, then went into accent and diction.

He was speaking with both lips stiffened and the chin nearly frozen when she nodded and whispered, "Yes, yes, that's him!"

Holding that same voice, he suggested, "But not exactly, right? Right, chick? There's no personality in this voice, is there? I mean—"

"Whine a little," she excitedly suggested. "Not overmuch, but sort of . . . sort of frustrated and mad at the same time, but you're trying to keep it under control."

"Right. Right, dolly. Whatta I got to do, honey, kick the hell right outta you? Is that what you want?"

Sara shivered. Her eyes dropped, and she told him, "That's just too real for comfort."

Bolan was guessing that it was no more than an approximation—but that was all most people heard, anyway. Something notable, something to hang an imperfect perception onto—it was that natural human frailty which made Bolan's masquerades possible.

She was asking him, "But what . . . why do you need . . . ?"

He told her, "Come and see."

They returned to the outside, and Sara stood stiffly in the drive, pointedly ignoring the crumpled bodies at her feet, as Bolan leaned into the vehicle and came out holding a microphone.

He smiled at her as he depressed the mike button, pulled on his "Hugger" face, and started his act. "Hey! Wake up!" he snarled.

A voice responded immediately from somewhere beneath the dashboard. "Who's that?"

"It's Little Red Riding Hood," Bolan replied nastily. "Skipping merrily through the goddamn countryside. Who the hell you think it is?"

"What you got, Hugger?"

Bolan tossed the girl a salute as he replied, "What does it sound like I got?"

"Okay, it's the same everywhere. Boss says go on to the next place. Waitaminnit! Hold it!"

Bolan told Sara in his own voice, "Maybe I blew it."

The other voice returned a moment later. "Okay, Hugger. Just got a report on th'other net. That farmer's on his way back, just came off the turnpike at Hightstown. We want you to stay there and check 'im out."

"What for?" Bolan/Hugger snarled back. "Smuggling chickenshit back into Jersey?"

"Boss says we check 'im coming and going, Hugger."

Bolan grimly smiled at Sara and replied, "Okay, but I think I'll meet 'im on the way. Gettin' dark soon. I don't wanta be out here in the dark with a daylight crew."

"Sure. Whatever makes you feel safe, Hugger."

It was a sarcastic sign-off.

Bolan was smiling coldly when he returned the microphone to its clip. He took the keys from the ignition and went around to open the trunk.

The girl followed him, questions in her eyes. "What was that all about?" she wanted to know.

"It's called covering tracks," he informed her. "When these boys come down missing in action, we don't want their buddies beginning the search here, do we?"

She soundlessly framed the reply "No" and moved out of his way as Bolan began the unpleasant task of stowing limp bodies and cleaning up gory evidence from the driveway. That job completed, he banged the lid on his cooling cargo, got into the car, and moved it to a place of concealment behind one of the sheds.

As he strode back to the house, he felt the spring

returning to his step, and he knew that his combat quickness was settling in on him again.

He was healed and ready for battle.

Almost ready.

Sara was waiting in the precise spot where he'd left her.

In a small voice she asked him, "What now, Mr. Bolan?"

"Now, love," he replied quietly, "we wait for the farmer. And his precious cargo from Manhattan."

The sun was disappearing into a red veil of smaze along the western horizon when Bruno Tassily wheeled his live-produce transporter with its empty cages into the farmyard.

The girl fled to her brother's arms and allowed herself a few luxurious tears as she greeted him; then she backed away, gave Bolan a somewhat embarrassed gaze, and ran into the house to quit that man's world for a while.

The men shook hands, and Bolan asked the big fellow, "How'd it go?"

"Directly on your numbers, Sarge," Bruno reported with a tired grin. "The stuff is in the tool well."

"Get it all?"

"Yeah. Uh, that Meyer boy . . . you didn't tell me. He's a double amputee. But, hell, he—"

"Yeah, he does all right, doesn't he?" Bolan said quietly.

"Like gangbusters, that's all. Uh, he gave me a message for you. Says business is booming all of a sudden, the past few days. Selling to guys he never heard of before. Says the word's out all over town.

They're recruiting guys right off the damn street corners. And he's having a run on guns like he never had before."

Bolan was smiling, but only with his lips. "Guns for Jersey, eh?"

"That's the impression Meyer has. He thinks they're fielding an army over here. And listen. I contacted that other friend of yours, too. He says . . . well, wait till we get inside. I have it written down."

They had moved on to the rear of the truck. Bruno was unlocking the tool compartment and ogling Bolan's black suit, apparently having just taken note of it. "Where'd you get that?" he asked.

"Sara made it," Bolan told him. "Quite a gal."

"You'll never know," Bruno said admiringly. "Sara has talents she hasn't even discovered yet."

Bolan could have told the big Romanian that his sister had discovered one or two that very day. Instead he said, "We had an incident, Bruno. Pretty unnerving for Sara. I had to shoot a couple of guys off her back. They're over behind your equipment shed, with their car. I'll be moving it away from here when it gets dark."

The big guy merely blinked his eyes at Bolan and began removing tools from the compartment. Then he got down to the part that counted, and Bolan began taking delivery of his new arsenal, checking it piece by piece as it came forth, grunting now and then with satisfaction over a particular item.

It required ten minutes to transfer the stuff to the shed. When they finally got into the house, Sara had coffee waiting, and the three of them sat at a small table near a window that provided an excellent view onto the roadway out front.

Bolan reminded his host about the "other message," and Bruno hastily whipped out a small notebook and began flipping the pages while the man in black quietly loaded clips with big ugly rounds of .44 magnum ammunition.

"Yeah, here it is," Bruno announced. "You'd never make it out. I better read it for you."

The message was from Leo Turrin, Bolan's secret comrade since almost the beginning of this war on the Mafia. Turrin was an underboss in a Massachusetts arm of the mob. He also was an undercover federal agent. Bolan scratched Leo's back, and he scratched Bolan's—in every way possible, and always at fantastic jeopardy to the man with the double life. It seemed as though it had been just days ago that the two of them had collaborated on Bolan's hazardous assignment in Philly. And then Leo had come in when Bolan needed his cooperation to accomplish the job in Sicily.

Stumbling as he deciphered his own notes, Bruno reported his conversation with Leo Turrin thus:

"He says you should lie low, don't move, don't even breathe hard. Federal marshals and state troopers are watching every highway and all public transportation facilities. Uh, and, yeah, he says to avoid all urban areas like the plague, especially, uh, the Jersey City and Newark areas. Cruise, uh . . . oh, he must have said *crews* . . . crews are coming down from all around the Northeast to plug Jersey solidly. They smell your blood. Know you're wounded and grounded somewhere. They're moving in for the kill. Says if you have to move, then move toward the sea. Long Beach, Asbury Park, that area. But even there you should count every grain of sand before you trust your foot to it. Uh . . . Marinello? Is that . . . ? Marinello is personally running the show. He takes it very personal what you did in Philly, as well as Sicily."

The big guy raised quizzical eyes to Bolan. "Who is Marinello?"

"Boss of all the bosses," Bolan said quietly.

Bruno shivered and took a quick sip of coffee before resuming the reading.

"He's got rolling command posts all over the area. Radio-equipped, with the smartest enforcers in his outfit personally directing the operations. Mike, uh, Talifero? . . . is also out somewhere in Jersey with a, uh, posse of headhunters, swearing to get you, or else he's not ever coming back."

Bolan chuckled at that, a chilling sound which momentarily clouded Sara's eyes.

"He says to give yourself a 'well done' for Philadelphia. The whole Angeletti family has fallen apart, or else at each other's throats, or else running clear out of the state. But he says to stay clear of Philly for now. The feds are looking for you to fall back in that direction, and they're primed and waiting for you to show."

Bolan lit a cigarette and blew the smoke into his hands.

"Also he said be sure to give you this report on Frank the Kid. Who's Frank the Kid, Sarge?"

"The heir to old man Angeletti's throne," Bolan explained.

"Well, not anymore. Here's what your guy said. Tell the Sarge that Frank the Kid was executed less than one hour after his arrival in New York. He got there with the wrong head."

The wondering eyes came up again to lock onto Bolan's expressionless gaze. "What does that mean? The wrong head?"

"He thought he had mine," Bolan said.

"Oh."

Sara quietly excused herself and hurried out of the room.

Bruno nervously shuffled the pages of his notebook and said, "That's it."

"Thanks," Bolan said. "Bruno, you're a hell of a guy."

"Forget Bruno," the Romanian replied in a very subdued voice. "What are *you*? How can you sit there all calm like that? Don't you know what I've just been telling you?"

"I know."

"You haven't a chance. Not a chance in a million."

"Guess I'll have to make one, Bruno."

"I . . . I know you can if anyone can, but . . ."

Bolan sighed, squeezed the big man's shoulder, and went to find Sara.

She was on the porch, arms folded across her bosom, staring morosely at the spot in the drive where she had been a close bystander to sudden and violent death.

He came up behind her and put his arms about her. "Don't let it bug you," he said, speaking softly with his lips at her ear.

"Why not?" she replied with a strangled little sigh. "That was no message. It was a sentence of death."

"I've had them before," he pointed out. "And I'm still here."

"Just barely." She sniffed.

His voice had a lilt to it as he reminded her, "That's not what you told me this afternoon."

She was very quietly and very unemotionally weeping. "Don't die, Mack," she said in a tiny voice. "Please, please don't die. Go back to the loft. We can keep you safe."

"No you can't. Each hour I spend here now is another fifty guns I'll have to face sooner or later."

"You don't *have* to—"

"Yes I do. You said something about a sentence of death. That sentence was pronounced a long time ago, Sara. The only way I avoid it is by shoving it back through their teeth. The minute I start trying to duck it, then I'm a dead man for sure. Besides . . ."

"Yes," she said in a tightening voice. "Finish it. Besides *what?* You *love* it, don't you? You're just *aching* to get back out there and . . . and—how did you say it?—shove it back in their teeth."

"Wish me well, Sara," he requested humbly.

"Oh . . . *God!*" she cried, twisting about and throwing her arms around him.

Yes, Him too, he thought bleakly.

Whatever and wherever You are, God, wish me well.

And suffer the young widows their solace.

5 COUNTERPOISE

He was in full combat rig.

The black suit that Sara had designed and built was a better fit than any he'd worn. It was made of an expanding, tough material that moved with him like his own skin; even the pockets hugged close until they were filled with something.

The Beretta Belle occupied her usual position of honor—shoulder-slung beneath the left arm. The AutoMag, fully armed and backed up, now rode heavy military web at his right hip.

A compact, folding-stock autopistol dangled free from a strap about his neck to ride loosely across his belly.

A miscellany of carefully selected munitions dangled from utility belts or lay snugly in the elastic pockets of the skinsuit. These included small fragmentation grenades, percussion pods, incendiaries, chemical smoke compressors, even a couple of small transistorized explosives.

Spare clips for the guns, a stiletto, and several small tools completed the ensemble.

Bruno looked the warrior over and commented, "You must be carrying a hundred pounds over your own weight."

"About that," Bolan agreed.

"Does the leg know it yet?"

"A little. But it'll get used to the idea."

"Just watch it," the worried Romanian cautioned in a curiously flattened voice. "Damnit, don't let them . . ." His voice broke. He spun about and marched stiffly toward the house.

Bolan stopped him with a quiet call, but the big guy did not turn all the way around.

"Bruno. You're a hell of a guy."

"Thanks. You too. Watch those *tocks*, eh."

"Name of the game," Bolan replied, chuckling.

Bruno went on, then, and Bolan stepped over to the vehicle.

He had carefully stowed the rest of his arsenal in the back-seat area and covered it with some empty feed sacks.

The two corpses remained in the trunk compartment.

A lovely young lady occupied a small portion of the front seat.

In a tinkly voice she asked him, "Are we ready to go?"

Gruffly he replied, "*We*, hell."

"I can run as fast as you."

"I'm not running, love," he quietly informed her.

"Well . . ."

Bruno burst back upon the scene at that moment, trotting from the rear of the house and waving a heavy money belt above his head.

"You forgot the war chest, Sarge!"

Bolan accepted the fat belt, stared at it for a moment, then shoved it back into Bruno's hands. "Hang on to it for me," he requested.

"You crazy? There's nearly a hundred thousand—"

"I took what I'll be needing for now. And if I don't make it through . . . well, can't take it with you, Bruno."

"Hey, Sarge, I can't—"

"Sure you can," the Executioner replied brusquely. He pulled the girl out of the car, slapped her lightly on the bottom, and told her, "All ashore."

She gasped, "Mack, I—"

He stopped her with a kiss, holding her deliciously close despite the intefering hardware.

When they came out of it, Bruno had disappeared.

Their eyes locked together, and a very special message quietly had its say there.

Then the girl's eyes fled that moment, and she told Bolan, "I-I'll always remember."

"Remember, too, what I told you this morning."

"I will," she whispered.

He slid into the car and closed the door.

"How did your husband die, Sara?" he gently asked her, through the window.

"I . . . they just said 'killed in action.' "

"Then he died living," the man in black told her. "I intend to do the same thing. But—damnit, Sara —you are a very special item. Promise me you won't live dying."

"Promise," she whispered. She wiped the moisture from her cheeks then, and told him, "The, uh, clothing you wore in here. It's all patched and pressed and hanging in the back window."

"Thanks, I noticed," he said, and then he kicked

the war wagon to life and quickly put that paradise behind him . . . and he did not look back.

The girl ran down the drive and stood there —a pathetic figure with slumped shoulders and dulled eyes—until the glow of his headlamps disappeared finally into the night.

She was walking dispiritedly toward the house when Bruno's truck lumbered around from the rear and gunned along the drive beside her.

She cried out, "Bruno! What are you . . . ?"

The truck rumbled on past and turned onto the road in Mack Bolan's wake.

Sara's hands went to her face, and she held that pose while tormenting thoughts and pictures spilled across her reeling consciousness.

Die living. Live dying. Kill, be killed. Fight, struggle, die, die, die, a million times die—what sort of world . . . ?

Remember what I told you this morning!

Yes, Sara, remember always.

"The universe must love you very much, Sara. Because you're a woman. And the female of every species is the universe in miniature, the living plasma of creation. She's the positive, uplifting force, the collector, the preserver, the nest-builder. You're the bridge of the generations, Sara. It's up to you to preserve what we men would destroy . . . without you."

Okay, sure, she could understand that kind of talk. Even from a relentless war machine like Mack Bolan. And he was more than that, of course. Much more. Yes. He was some kind of man.

She straightened her shoulders and turned back toward the house.

Okay, Mother Sara, preserver of the races and wife of the universe. Get in there and start nesting.

She went inside, turned on all the lights, put the Tijuana Brass on the hi-fi, found her sketchpad, and began designing herself a new summer wardrobe.

6 DRAW PLAY

"What you got, Hugger?"

"A suspicious. Just off Thirty-three by the fair-grounds. I don't wanta go down in there with just me 'n' the kid. Some guy's camping down there, fire and everything."

"Where'd you say that is?"

"A box canyon on this little road just east of the fairgrounds, by that new interstate."

"Our sectionals don't show no box canyon around there, Hugger."

"Well, damnit, you better look again! I'm telling you . . . Whuup! Change that, it's no *suspicious!* It's him, it's the guy! You get me some help here damn quick!"

"Boss says damnit you sit tight! Don't try nothing on your own. We're on the way!"

"I'm sittin'! But you shag ass!"

Bolan smiled a smile that was not a smile and thumbed off the microphone. All he had to do now was to wait. And he'd learned, long ago, to wait.

He had traveled not east from the Tassily farm, but west—clear to the approaches of Trenton; and he'd found his battle site near a place called Mercerville, not far from the state fairgrounds.

The terrain here was not the most ideal, but he had desired to get as far west as feasible, hoping to draw the hounds away from the trails he planned to travel later that evening.

And he'd found a pretty decent site for a fire trap—more or less remote, a bit of woods, some open area with a bit of high ground overlooking it . . . and an escape path to the rear.

He had covered the area thoroughly in a walking recon, in the dark; then he'd built a small campfire at dead center, dumped his cargo of cold meat and carefully laid it out just so, then moved the vehicle to the elevated land overlooking the scene.

The target range would be about fifty yards. It would be a hellish lay for those foolish enough to be caught down there.

Before summoning the foolish ones, he carefully investigated the back way out, found it passable in the vehicle, then returned immediately to the fire trap and began setting up.

He positioned infrared floods and took range-finder readings from three different locations on the ridge, then set up a couple of LAWs (light anti-tank weapons) and made them ready, put some heavy grenades out, checked his personal weapons . . . and went to the radio to spread some blood for the shark pack.

At this range the LAW would do about anything a bazooka could do, and Bolan had a couple of special missions in mind for those deadly dudes.

He also had a honey of a new nighttime sniper piece which had come from the William Meyer & Company "munitions-at-a-price" supermarket in Manhattan—and at a very dear price.

Meyer was more than an illicit arms dealer. He was also a physically shattered survivor of Vietnam, a skilled armorer like Bolan, and a genius at modifying old arms to newfangled kill specifications.

A lifetime victim of warfare, Meyer had found a way to make the human proclivity for destruction pay off in a particularly ironic and profitable fashion . . . or so he'd told Bolan at the height of the nightmare in New York. Meyer had discovered that munitions makers do not take sides in small wars; they merely build destruction to specification for whatever damn fools want to come along and set it loose upon the world.

Hinting, of course that Bolan was one of the damn fools.

Bolan had never argued with the man. Damn fool or not, he had a job that needed doing, and there seemed to be no one else around who was ready, able, or willing to take it on. It just happened that Bolan had all three of those qualifications; and here he was—damn fool, maybe—but here nevertheless, on a Jersey hillside in the dead of night, waiting his chance to let loose quite a ration of destruction upon the world of damn fools.

And the foolish ones came, recklessly, straining at the bit like so many excited bloodhounds with scent strong in their nostrils, tearing along that lonely road down there like the hounds of hell had done since the beginning of life.

Two vehicles, then a third, and finally a stream-lined van sort of thing—one of those houses on wheels which gentler people used to get back to nature without really suffering. And now Bolan knew

47

what the boys were utilizing for their "rolling command posts."

The mob, too, liked their comforts. Even on kill missions.

He let them come, and watched the two lead vehicles jounce into that clearing and tear off on opposing circular paths toward the far end. The third car was a standard crew wagon. It came on through the slot and halted just inside; doors popped open; energetic men found their feet and their weapons in a quick debarkation and an even quicker fanning out across that clearing.

Then the camper came down, halting right in the slot and squatting there with lights ablaze.

Pretty damned confident, Bolan was thinking.

Still, damned effective. He'd had a hard time counting heads and keeping track of the maneuvers as well.

He had actually seen twelve heads. There were probably at least twenty, not counting whoever was in that command van.

All four vehicles had left their headlamps on high beams, and they were taking up positions to flood that entire clearing with light.

Bolan grinned and leaned into the first LAW.

He lined up the pop sights onto the steering wheel of that glass-fronted van just as an excited shout from down by the campfire advised everyone present, *"Here they are, both dead!"*

"So where's their car?" This, an amplified voice of authority from a loudspeaker mounted somewhere on the van. The man was in there, some man with rank.

And the dismal reply from the campfire: "Forget it, the guy's gone. I guess he's got their car now."

"Correction," Bolan sighed as he squeezed the little missile out of the tube. "The guy has not gone."

The AP rocket whizzed along its beeline of destruction and impacted precisely where Bolan had sent her, and she came in with a happy hurrah and a mushroom of flames as glass, metal, and all else in that immediate vicinity stood aside, and departed, and gave over the night to this ill-behaved and uninvited guest.

Bolan abandoned the throwaway tube and took up his next firedrop as panic erupted down there, and screams, shouts, and startled commands rushed in to fill the void.

He hit them with a heavy grenade, dead center in the campfire, following immediately with another directly on the front bumper of the crew wagon; and now the pandemonium was in full sway.

"Turn off them goddamn lights!"

"Oh, shit, shit . . . help me!"

"Boss! Boss! Al is blowed all to hell and I . . ."

"Up there! The bastard's up . . ."

Bolan was into the nighttime sniper, jaw tightened and twitching as he bent to the infrared nightscope, and the big piece began jolting his shoulder as scurrying men stumbled into his cross hairs and catapulted out of them.

There were no blazing headlamps down there now—just blazes period as here and there scattered firebrands from the campfire plus small fires in the two rearward vehicles lent ghastly relief to the ever-growing carnage of the night.

49

Bolan's sniper was cracking methodically in evenly spaced retorts to the chattering of automatic weapons off there in the darkness. The invisible infrared floods were doing their bit for the moment, painting the scene ghoulish as viewed through the sniperscope. Bullets sprayed the trees behind him, chewed turf and chipped rock all below him; still the big piece continued its chilling toll of the night, while men screamed, and wondered aloud how he was spotting them, and pleaded for assistance from gods who knew not their names, and simply yelled foul imprecations upon their fate.

And, after a while, Bolan switched off his infrareds, stowed his gear, and made his withdrawal in an eerie silence.

He stopped briefly at a service station on Route Thirty-three, stepped onto the service ramp in full combat regalia, and suggested to two pop-eyed attendants that someone call the police.

He swung immediately northward from there, found the little state road that connects Mercerville to Edinburg, and made fast tracks toward the sea.

So, okay. It had been hellish . . . but not entirely damn-foolish. Maybe he would succeed in drawing some of the opposing guns this way.

So call it eight hundred Jersey guns waiting for him now.

He smiled faintly into the enshrouding night.

The odds were coming down.

7 THE GAME NAMED

He had been running the back roads, carefully avoiding major routes and intersections, and his instincts had drawn him past the toll road at Cranbury and on south of Prospect Plains, from where he hoped to angle on eastward to Freehold, thence on to the coast via Neptune.

This would set him down roughly midway between New York and Atlantic City, with an endless selection of small coastal towns from which to work another angle of escape.

Twice he had narrowly avoided a confrontation with police authority, and twice he had sent up a shaky thanks to whatever powers controlled chance and circumstance.

Running head-on into elements of the outfit was one thing; into the cops, quite another. Mack Bolan did not fight cops. They were "soldiers of the same side." His only defense from that quarter lay in studious avoidance.

And now he was thinking that it would be wise to give the enemy—and the police—some reaction time *vis-à-vis* the hit near Mercerville. Already, it seemed, he was encountering cross-currents or pursuit in that direction. A wise warrior knew when to strike, when to retreat, and when to simply lie low.

Thus it was that the Executioner elected to seek a snug harbor for a brief period of détente. It was a matter of pure coincidence that he found that harbor just a few miles to the north of the Tassily farm, near a sleeping village called Tennent.

It was a trailer camp with a weathered sign announcing a rather unemotional welcome for "Campers and Overnighters—All Hookups Available."

The place was all but deserted; apparently its season had not yet arrived.

It boasted a public rest room and shower, an all-night laundromat, a couple of picnic tables just off the roadway, several rows of unoccupied trailer spaces, and a small office building with a single dull bulb over the door with instructions to "Ring for Service."

All Bolan desired was a secluded place to park awhile—but not too secluded—and he felt no need to "ring" for anything. He angled the vehicle in the rear of the public buildings, appropriately positioned for a quick out, and spent ten minutes or so studying the detailed maps that had come with the car. One of these was singularly revealing, seeming to pinpoint "patrol zones" and specific rendezvous areas.

He tucked the intelligence away for possible future consideration, loath now to abandon the plan he already had cooking.

Then he spotted the public phone booth in the shadows of the laundromat, briefly debated a call to New York . . . and lost the debate.

He pulled the car closer to the phone booth and

a few minutes later was speaking into a connection to a fashionable hotel in midtown Manhattan.

"This is Al La Mancha," he told the familiar voice at the far end. "I gotta talk to Mr. Turrin; it's very important."

"This is Turrin," came the cautious reply. "Who'd you say that is?"

"Al La Mancha. Listen, this is pretty hot stuff."

"Uh . . . look, Al. I was just going out. Why don't you try me in a little while, at, uh . . ."

It was a familiar routine. These contacts with the most wanted dude in the country were potentially disastrous for "the man from Mass" who rode two steeds through the jungle called life. To preclude any deadly compromise of his cover, as well as to shield him from possible official embarrassment at the other side, the friendship with Mack Bolan was necessarily a furtive thing. Early in the wars, therefore, they had worked out the contact routine.

Bolan knew that Turrin was at this moment digging for the number of a nearby public telephone, which he quickly found and relayed to "La Mancha" —a sort of comic-relief code name for Mack Bolan.

Early in his wars, some segments of the press had taken to referring to Bolan as "a latter-day Don Quixote"—the fabled windmill-slayer of another grim era of man's misadventures. Therefore, "the man from La Mancha."

Precisely five minutes following that hang-up, Bolan had another quick connection.

"That you, La Mancha?" asked the voice of the truest friend the Executioner had ever known.

"It's me. Where are you, Leo?"

"Downstairs, basement lobby. It's okay. What's your situation?"

"About normal," Bolan replied, trying to keep the voice light. Leo Turrin was a worrier.

"Then you haven't been hearing the words I've been getting," came the taut response. "I'm not going to ask you where you are, and I don't want you to tell me. Just tell me this: are you anywhere near Mercerville?"

Bolan chuckled as he replied, "The word's out, then."

"Yeah, and so is everything else," was the wry rejoinder. "You really know how to stir the pot, Sarge. I hope you hit and ran like hell."

"I did."

Turrin sighed heavily, and Bolan heard the snap of a cigarette lighter close to the mouthpiece. "It came as quite a shock. The heads all thought you were down and just awaiting the final count. Tell the truth, I'd started wondering along those lines myself until your friend contacted me today. By the way—"

"He's okay, Leo. But I hope you covered your end."

"Oh, sure. I caught the coded flicker and knew right away he was a stand-in. Don't worry, he never knew who he was talking to. Anyway, what I was about to say . . . a guy by the name of Tassily walked into a state police substation tonight and . . . Is this the same guy, Sarge?"

Very quietly Bolan said, "Same guy, Leo."

"Well, don't sound so . . . Hear me out. The guy claims he's been a prisoner of the Executioner these past few days—he and his sister—on a chicken farm or something they have down mid-state. The Jersey fuzz don't know whether to buy his story or not. They're out at that farm right now, sifting the place down for some back-up. Anyway, Tassily says you're springing southward. Claims you've been studying maps of lower Jersey, particularly that area down below Wharton State Forest. Says he thinks your ultimate goal is Delaware Bay, where he hints you've got a boat stashed."

Bolan was chuckling now. "Some kind of guy," was all he said.

"Yeah, well, that's privately the way Hal and I look at it. We guessed the guy is trying to lead the chase down a dead end."

"You're in present contact with Hal Brognola?"

"Yeah. He's pushing the federal troops, from here in New York for the moment."

"Give him my best. And tell him not to crowd me too much for now. I have plenty to occupy my time as it is."

The undercover fed was chuckling. "You know how Hal feels about you. But there are plenty of mixed emotions there, buddy. He's got about a dozen top-level bureaucrats just laying all over him. If they ever get the notion that he's dogging it, even a little . . . well, you know."

"Yeah, I know. I respect the guy for doing his job, Leo. Well . . . I better—"

"Wait, don't be so touchy. Listen, now, nobody is offering you a license or anything like that, but . . . well, Hal is advising the local officials to buy Tassily's story. It's as good a lead as any they've had. Also, Hal threw in that bit of past history where you seem to favor escapes by sea. He cited the escape at Los Angeles, the one at Miami, in France, the recent one down in Washington where you had a boat stashed on the Potomac. . . ."

Bolan sighed and agreed. "I guess it fits."

"Sure it does. Simple police logic. And the hit at Mercerville fits like a hand in the glove. The Jersey troopers are considering rushing everything they can spare into a coverage along U. S. 206 South. That's the fast route to Wharton. They're spread pretty thin already. So . . . But I guess they'll buy Tassily. Need I say more?"

"There's one very large fly," Bolan quietly decided.

"And what is that?"

"The *boys* won't buy Tassily. They've been laying over that farm like a mother hen all this week. They've seen the guy going and coming freely, and they were in there several times on a shakedown. His story won't hold water in their bag, that's sure. You'd better get the guy and his sister out of there, Leo. Protective custody or whatever it takes to keep them covered until this thing blows over."

"Yes, I see your point. Okay. I'll get on that as soon as I hang up."

"Tell me something, Leo. With cops crossing tracks all over this damn state, how is the mob operating so openly? They're running regular armed convoys around here."

Turrin released a hissing sigh, and Bolan knew that he was in for a classroom discussion. "You've never spent much time in Jersey," the undercover man pointed out. "You couldn't know . . . well, it's a most unusual state, let's put it that way. The sent administration is going through all manner of nightmares trying to correct the . . . well, it's just a horrendous mess. The problem is as much geography as anything. The whole place lies in the shadow of New York and Pennsylvania—almost completely overshadowed. The greater population is massed along those borders, with Philly and New York City providing more of a swing to the state than anything Jersey can get together within her own borders. That urban mass up around Newark and Jersey City is actually feudal states within their own right—and that's just an accentuation of the general problem everywhere in the state. The corruption is just . . . well, don't let me start on that. Just get this understanding, buddy. You are in the heartland, the mob's green acres, and if they want to chase you around in armed convoys, don't think for a minute there's anyone to really oppose them."

"Okay. That fits my reading."

"Sarge, there's not even a national television outlet into that state. The people of Jersey get their contact with the outer world via Philly, Bethlehem, and New York City. They don't even have a newspaper with statewide circulation."

"Yeah, I get that. A state without a state. You say the present governor is—"

"He's trying," Turrin replied, sighing. "But then, there's all that cloud from beyond the borders, and the very real political power of the city-states."

"Well. Maybe I'll look around some while I'm here."

"Good Christ! I was afraid you were starting to lean that way! Perish the very thought, Sarge."

"I hear that Augie Marinello is leading the charge this time."

"He is. From here, though, on his fat ass."

"I guess he's a bit unhappy over Philly."

"In spades. By the way, you can forget the *gradigghia,* for now anyway. Augie got your message from Sicily. He put out an edict yesterday. No more imported guns. He was simply appalled by the slaughter in the Old Country."

"I see. What you are telling me—"

"I'm telling you that you did a good job in Sicily. Next time why don't you just take a quiet ocean cruise."

"Okay," Bolan replied, sighing. He lit a cigarette and listened to Leo Turrin's tight breathing for a charged moment; then he said, "I'd rather go into an operation with a bit more visibility . . . but . . . I guess I'm here, aren't I?"

"Aw, no, Sarge. No. Come back if you want, and I'll help you set up some solid intel. But not now. There's just too much working against you. Get out and take some R and R."

"It just tears my guts, Leo. To think of these guys running around like savages, lord of the domain, doing whatever they damn please."

"I know how you feel. Hell. But you've survived this far on cool, Mack. Go on surviving, damnit. We need you. This whole dog-eat-dog world needs you. Hey. I can talk to you like that, can't I?"

Bolan chuckled. "Sure. What's happening up north?"

"Newark-Jersey City? About two hundred guns are happening, I'd say. Manning the ramparts into New York. Don't try it."

"I get the feeling you're nudging me somewhere, Leo."

"Try Atlantic City, Sarge."

"Why?"

"Because there's a boat headed that way. It's the *Lotta Linda*. Off the boardwalk, north. Steel Pier. Anytime after midnight."

Bolan chuckled again. "You're so damn cute. Well, I'll give it a look. Thanks, Leo. Uh, don't forget the chicken ranch."

"I'll get right on it. Stay hard, man."

"Name of the game," Bolan said quietly, and hung up.

He signaled the operator and settled his overtime charges, then returned to his vehicle, deep in thought.

The name of the game, he thought, wryly, was *beat it!*

But . . . he was just a few miles north of the farm.

If there was the slightest chance of . . .

After all his pains to cover his tracks around that place . . . Well, Bruno couldn't be expected to know. It was all Bolan's doing, anyway. He'd leaked in there and talked the guy out of passive living, and if the guy was in a mess now, then it was Bolan's mess, not Bruno's. Certainly not Sara's.

Some nightmares had an uncomfortable propensity for coming true.

And Bolan just could not shake from his head that latest twist in skin-crawling dreams—that one wherein a chicken ranch becomes a horror-farm of screaming turkeys.

Leo was right, too, of course. He simply was not ready for a Jersey operation.

As sure as God made lush green valleys, though,

the Executioner would be returning to Jersey one day . . . prepared!

He fired up the war wagon and kicked her southward.

For now, he could run past the Tassily farm, reassure his mind, then angle on down to Atlantic City. It was the only route of sanity.

Or so he thought.

New routes, beyond Bolan's immediate power of manipulation, were at that very moment being plowed by the Jersey guns.

8 FROM THE TREETOP

He cruised by the Tassily farm in a slow pass, taking a reading of the situation there.

A police car was in the drive, beacon flashing; another was pulled more toward the rear of the place, out by the sheds, no lights showing except an interior lamp, the driver's door standing open.

The house was lit up all over, as were the outbuildings. The yard floodlights were on.

But he had seen not one thing moving back there, no signs of life whatever.

The scene struck him as unnatural.

He seesawed across the road and went back, pulling into the drive with headlamps extinguished and motor idling.

Then he saw it, the thing in the driveway beside the police cruiser—a crumpled human form.

He descended into that place with all his senses flaring into the alert.

There was not a sound about, except for the faint whirr-click of the cruiser's beacon and a muffled squawking from its radio.

The uniformed trooper was lying face-down in the drive. He had been shot in the back of the head. He was dead.

The vehicle in back was a sheriff's car. He found the two deputies by the brooder house. Also shot dead.

Bolan came upon the live one inside the house. A state trooper, young, twenty-five maybe, with a bullet in the gut and suffering like hell.

He knelt over the guy and asked him, "You okay?"

The cop's eyes flared into that confrontation with the man in black, and he groaned, "I *was.*"

"Then you still are," the Executioner assured him.

He broke out a battle compress, sprinkled it with antibiotic powder, and applied it to the wound.

"Hold it down tight," he suggested. "You'll make it if you can stand the pain. What happened here?"

"Gunmen," the cop replied through gritted teeth. "Surprised us . . . took Tassily and . . . his sister."

"How long?" Bolan asked, in a voice pitched from hell.

"Not . . . long. Few minutes at most."

"What were they driving?"

The young officer's look was an even mixture of pain and self-disgust. "That's the . . . dumb part. Big camper. You know . . . these . . . Land Rover things. Who would've thought . . . ?"

Bolan said, "Okay, don't push it. I'll get you some help. Did you see which way they went out of here?"

"Sounded like . . . up the road."

Bolan was rising to take departure when the cop's hand flopped over to pull weakly at his arm. "Those guys . . . they're . . . worst kind. Camper wasn't all. Two limousines came in . . . after. They wanted those people . . . worst way."

"So do I," the Executioner grimly assured the cop; then he pulled away and hurried out of there.

He paused briefly at the cruiser out front and got on the police radio. "Officer in trouble," he reported. "Tassily farm, you know where. Send an ambulance, and scream it!"

The police dispatcher wasted no time over technicalities. He obviously "knew where" very well.

Bolan ignored the terse requests for further information and put that place quickly behind him.

And, yes, the hounds from hell had barked up a very mean tree this time.

Mack Bolan was deadly enough in his most passive moments.

And now that black-clad doomsday guy was seething with anger, trembling with determination, the usually expressionless face twisted into a torment of anxiety and utter resolution.

The hounds were to discover very quickly that they had tried to tree a dragon.

Bolan knew this jungle well, and he knew how to read the signs left there. He found the fresh impressions left by the heavy van as it cornered too tightly onto the back road to Trenton, and he found other signs beyond there which told of a gleeful and reckless joyride toward the headshed of local power.

Once he thought he'd actually caught a glimpse of their lights on a curve far ahead, but the terrain was working against him this time.

He swung away from the track a few miles east of the next junction and gambled on a cross-country plunge along a narrow dirt trail which, he hoped, would put him somewhere out front of the turkey-land express.

It did, and he was, and he met them at that back-country crossroads in the moonless night with perhaps fifteen seconds of advance preparation.

He was lined and targeted into the crossroads itself, and he met them there as they flew through in convoy procession, the two crew wagons leading.

The first car through the target zone took a LAW hit on the forward door post, exploded immediately into flames, and went into a cartwheel down that narrow road.

Car number two was already into the wreckage of the first casualty and pulling like hell for freedom when the next rocket slammed into her rear quarter. She went to ground on an expansive cushion of flame, then blew straight up with raining droplets of fiery gasoline and settled in a screeching heap directly in the path of the oncoming van.

The van jockey was already pulling brakes with everything he had, and now he overreacted with a lunging turn on locked brakes and blew through the flaming wreckage in a broadside skid that ended abruptly and disastrously with the rear section wrapped around a steel light standard.

A secondary exposion rocked the remains of the first car and flung shards of heavy glass and metal all about that disaster zone at the same moment that the camper came to rest.

Bolan, however, was like a homing missile with but one objective in mind. Totally ignoring the crew wagons and what was left of their passengers, he walked through that raining chaos with the big silver AutoMag thrust forward at chest level, headed unerringly for the turkey wagon, and the first man to come stumbling out of there was met in the doorway with 240 grains of exploding fire power right in the center of the forehead.

Another was trying to eject a revolver through a twisted porthole; the AutoMag again roared massive anger, and a mutilated hand was quickly jerked back inside.

He did not wait for the debarkation, but went in after them. The driver was bent over the steering wheel in his luxuriously padded seat, hands clasped to a bleeding face. Bolan jerked the head back, thrust the snout of the silver pistol through clenched teeth, and blew that fucking head off.

Another guy was seated at a small table just down the aisle, except that now the table was riding the guy's chest and pinning him to the wall. The butt of a pistol was showing from one of the guy's pockets, but he was too stunned even to go for it.

Bolan left him with a grotesque third eye that made the three as one as he passed on into the interior.

He found the "boss"—a guy he vaguely recognized as one of the top torpedoes out of Marinello's Manhattan head shop—emerging from a curtained-off area at about midships.

The guy was dragging Sara Henderson along in front of him—a thoroughly terrified and bug-eyed Sara—and he was bleeding all down the front of her from the shattered hand that pinned her to him.

The other hand held a pistol at her head, and the guy was yelling, "Okay, now! Watch it, Bolan!"

Bolan watched it.

He watched a 240 grain extension of cold fury

plow right past Sara's pink little ear to splatter that ugly face behind it, leaving not even a dying reflex to tickle that trigger at her head.

For the second time that day, Bolan had shot a monster off that girl's back, and he felt utterly miserable about the whole thing.

She was undoubtedly feeling rather miserable, herself. The dress was torn half away from her. Ugly splotchy bruises marred that lovely skin in every place that showed, and her eyes were absolutely wild.

She collapsed into his arms and nestled her head on his shoulder as he carried her out of that hellbox.

"Where's Bruno?" he asked as soon as they reached open air.

"Gone," she moaned. "They took him."

"He wasn't with you?"

"Not now."

He gazed toward the fiery limousines and told her in a choked voice, "In this game, it's all or nothing, Sara. I had to go for the numbers."

Bad off as she was, she noted the anguish in him and hastened to tell him, "No! Not there! They took him away, some other cars."

Well . . . that was good, and it was bad.

Good because there was still a chance for Bruno. But a mighty slim one.

Bad because sudden death in an exploding vehicle just beat the shivers out of the slow but certain lingering reality of a turkey-style interrogation.

"Don't faint, Sara! Suck in your gut and chuck it up if you have to. Scream, cuss, call me names, whatever ticks you. But damnit, don't faint! You've got to help me find Bruno!"

"Don't worry about me, Mack Bolan." The voice was tiny but firm. "I understand you now, your war. I truly understand."

Yes, Sara had been through some hell, herself.

But she was fighting back. God love her, she was fighting back.

9 THE UNDERSTANDING

There was more pain for Sara than problem—pain and a rather jarring loss of feminine composure.

The boys had not been too rough on her—a bit of pinching in sensitive places and slapping around, routine terrorizing.

They'd fondled her where no man had a right to without permission, and indulged in some low street-corner humor and wisecracks.

The really rough stuff would have come later.

Bolan took her to his vehicle, where he gave her a canteen of water and some gauze with which to swab away the blood and other washable marks she'd collected from the dead torpedo. Not much could be done about the welts and bruises she'd picked up before that; only time.

He left her there in privacy and went back for a quick shakedown of the command van.

A surface search of the vehicle and its crew left him with very little of useful intelligence. A couple of maps, some identities, a few odds and ends that might come together later.

When Bolan returned to his own vehicle, Sara was cleanly composed and ready to travel. He took one last look at the site where God or something had intervened in that girl's fate; then he burned rubber away from that place, leaving flaming wreckage and cooking bodies behind.

Most people, he knew, would find it difficult to believe the depth of horror that had been awaiting Sara Henderson on that bleak Jersey night. Sara herself would not have believed.

Everyday people simply had no mental concept of the deeper depravities that stalked this tired old earth.

Memories of places like Buchenwald and other infamies faded all too quickly from the human experience.

Bolan knew. His "memories" had been kept up to date.

It would not have mattered that Sara had already told the turkey-makers everything she knew, which she had. She'd seen no reason to conceal the truth. She had thought Bolan well clear of the area. And she told them all of it, a couple of times.

No matter if they had been convinced that she'd told all—even that would not have saved her.

The "talk-turkey" theory differed from brain washing and other gentler techniques in that it featured a greatly accelerated and heightened approach—not brain *washing,* but brain *busting.*

The technique was based on the idea that human perception and recall is a tricky and often deceptive thing. It followed (quite by accident) the same psychological reasoning as the more socially acceptable "encounter-group" techniques of emotional release. Bits of intelligence could be hidden in the subconscious as involuntarily as could bits of destructive emotions and psychic trauma. The art of turkey-making, however, was far older than the quasi-science of human psychology, and much more effective.

The "encounter-group" technique of psychotherapy amounted to a voluntary submission to emotional shock and nonphysical torture.

Turkey-talk "therapy" was aimed toward the same result, but with a much more straightforward approach, and a much quicker result.

Though the various steps of the technique had never been formulated into a precise discipline, the practice of the art went somewhat along these lines:

Begin with fear and terror, threats, promises of severe physical suffering.

Then induce actual physical pain, gradually. Get the victim to screaming and pleading for mercy.

A lot of stuff would come flinging out of the mind right there, at that point, a lot of stuff the victim never even knew was there.

So, induce more pain. A hell of a lot more. Get the entire physical ststem involved in it, until the victim is flopping about all over the place and yelling his head off.

So, keep it up. More, more, and then a hell of a lot more . . . until the poor bastard has reached the absolute limit of human endurance. Watch the whole damn nervous system collapse, and listen to what pops out of that.

But keep him conscious and aware. Let off for a little while, give the strength a chance to build back. Then do it again, all the way; get him back up there, and keep prodding until something new splits loose.

Let off again. Be nice. Smile at the suffering shit.

But watch how he shrinks back each time you make a gesture in his direction; listen to how he screams if you so much as touch him with a finger. Now you're getting into the guy; you're almost there.

So, hit him now with massive shock. Confound the very soul, fragment it, send it screaming through hell. If the turkey is a guy, cut off his cock. If a broad, slice off a tit or shove a busted Coke bottle up her snatch.

And listen to all the shit pouring out now.

And the time has arrived when you can become *really* creative.

Hit them in their hottest spot. If the guy happens to be a surgeon or a piano player, for example, off with his goddamn fingers . . . one by one. Show them to him, play catch with them, shove 'em up his ass. But keep him alive. Get a blowtorch or something and cauterize those stumps.

It could go on and on like that, taking the guy apart in pieces, for as long as he could be kept aware and screaming and alive.

All kinds of shit would pour out, maybe even how he screwed Maryjane in the sandbox at kindergarten. These slobs got so goddamn anxious to tell you everything they knew, everything they could conceivably know and not know, they even started inventing stuff, making it up, trying to find something to satisfy you so you'd stop.

But you didn't stop.

You never stopped until the guy stopped.

You kept right on busting through that brain, shredding that soul, dissolving that personality into scattered bits and pieces; and you kept that poor shit talking turkey until he talked himself dead.

That was the technique.

And if you were a real artisan, a really masterful turkey-maker, you could probably keep something like that going around the clock. Some guys in Chicago had once kept it going for more than three days. Of course, in all fairness to the other masters, they'd had a three-hundred-pound turkey to work with.

Sara, by the grace of God, had been spared that.

Bruno could still be facing it.

But not if there was anything beneath God's heaven which Bolan could do to prevent it.

Mack Bolan was a mighty tough guy—*genuinely* tough, in the spirit, where it counted.

He could steel himself to almost anything. But he could not steel himself into an acceptance of turkey meat.

He would have killed his own mother, quickly and without regret, before he would allow her to fall into a turkey-maker's hands.

And he would quickly do the same for Bruno Tassily, if that was the last resort.

He had not thought it necessary to explain such things to Sara. He had not told her *why* he so quickly, and with such seeming recklessness, had twice that day placed her under the fire of his own guns.

But, in some vague fashion, Sara understood; he knew that. She had received only the merest hint of what could have lain in store for her that night, but it was hint enough and she had made a point to let him know quickly that she understood.

Bolan could only hope that Sara's understanding would never become complete.

Not every *mafioso* was a turkey-maker, of course.

Even the meanest of the button men sometimes turned green if someone even mentioned turkey to them. It took a genuine sadist, a really sick mind, to pull that kind of duty, even as an assistant.

So, there were the specialists.

Mike Talifero, it had been said, had a full assortment of such "specialists," and Bolan would bet a million bucks that each of those command vans cruising the Jersey hellgrounds that night was carrying a Talifero specialist.

These guys were out here to collect the Executioner's head, and they meant to have it.

They would stop at nothing . . . and nobody.

And how they would love to get Mack Bolan's brain to bust, his soul to shred. Just for fun.

That idea did not particulary bother the man in black. He would live until he died; and if he died screaming, well, okay. Bolan did not contemplate his own death.

He contemplated the death of others. Those who roamed and ranged and plundered the human estate, those who degraded life itself and sucked out dignity and meaning and hope.

Yes. He contemplated their deaths even in his sleep.

He would contemplate their deaths even while he himself was dying.

And if Sara understood *that,* then she'd done a bit of brain busting on her own—but in a much, much gentler fashion.

10 THE SITUATION

Bolan's modus operandi was slipping badly.

He was a hellfire guy, hit and git, disappear quickly, pop up again at some far-removed spot to hit and fade again. It was guerrilla warfare, and it had kept his hide intact through fifteen major encounters with this enemy.

But now, here in Jersey, the whole game had changed in a most disheartening manner.

He was running around in tight circles, highly visible, with very little design and no plan whatever.

Certainly he was not on a battleground of his own choosing.

Jersey had been on his hit list, sure. But not for this particular point in time. Mainly because it was much too close to one of his most recent theaters of operation.

At first Jersey had been an escape route, not—to his mind—a field for combat. He liked to pick them a bit more carefully than that.

But also he was not prepared for a war with the Jersey mob. In the first place, there was no Jersey mob, *per se*. The guys up around Newark and Jersey City were hardly more than an arm of the New York group, especially since their ranking member on La Commissione had started getting his tail salted by the feds.

A couple other New York outfits had the Port of New York under contest, including the Jersey side of it.

Trenton, the capital city, had its own special problems, not a few of which were caused by old Stefano Angeletti, the fading boss of Philly, plus varied and sundry oddfellows from just about every Mafia interest in the Northeast United States.

New Jersey was not only a state without a state; it was also a mob without a mob.

The entire area was a refuse bin for everything the states of New York and Pennsylvania wished to toss over—including their underworld garbage.

Leo Turrin had not been exaggerating when he described the problem as a "horrendous mess."

It was easily that.

Bolan was beyond being amazed at the capacity for American citizens to accept the clearly unacceptable.

But he had always felt a bit numbed with every glance at the state of New Jersey.

The situation here was more than horrendous. It was appalling.

So . . . no. Bolan was not prepared to tackle New Jersey. If the Mafia was an octopus, then Jersey was an octopus whose tentacles were detached and wriggling about the entire landscape on independent and all-encompassing feedings.

Bolan would need a very close-cadence group of numbers to tackle an enemy like that. And that meant painstaking intelligence, planning, logistics, a very precise battle strategy.

At the moment, Bolan was no more than another piece of garbage flung onto the Jersey soil.

His only desire had been to get the hell out of there.

Bruno Tassily and his sister had made it possible for him to achieve that objective. And, sure, he could have done so, without too much sweat, by simply playing his game his way.

Following the diversion hit at Mercerville, he could have scooted free and clear to the coast, and probably, at this very moment, be floating down the Atlantic to freedom and better battlefields.

Very probably he could still do so.

But it would be a "freedom" totally without meaning.

Bolan was not a glory guy. And he was not fighting merely to remain alive. The thing went much deeper than that, into an area of the human dimension which Bolan could not put words to.

Nothing in life could be measured in precise terms of right and wrong, good and bad, black and white. He knew that. And he knew how corny it sounded to talk about "good versus evil," and the like.

Bolan had discovered, though, that things usually become "corny" only because they are so universally applicable—the "true" does have an annoying way of becoming commonplace, mainly because it has such durability.

But he also understood that "evil" was self-propelling, and much stronger than passive "good." That latter condition needed a bit of propellant itself if it was going to remain in the race with the other.

Maybe Edmund Burke was simply being "corny"

when he declared, "The only thing necessary for the triumph of evil is for good men to do nothing."

But Mack Bolan agreed with that statement, corny or not.

Bolan *lived* that philosophy, cornball or not.

He did not respect meaningless freedom.

He did not cherish "life at any price."

He did, though, very strongly wish to spring a friend from the shadows of hell.

And he would, by God, do so, if there was any way under the sun.

That was the entire damned "situation" of the moment.

11 THROUGH THE MAZE

"There were three cars," Sara explained. "I remembered the importance of . . . I pretended I had a pad and that I was sketching it all. Tried to burn it into my mind as vividly as possible. There was a sports car, some foreign make. I never could tell one from the other, except this was an expensive type. Then there were two big cars, Cadillacs I guess, the kind with the folding jump seats, gleaming black.

"The men all looked very hard, brutal. Except the one. He got out of the sports car, with another man. He was . . . well, handsome in a way. A little older than you, Mack. About the same general physique, except an inch or so shorter than you. Very expensively dressed, very sharp. A blue double-knit suit with flared legs, wide lapels. Most beautiful shirt I've ever seen . . . I couldn't even guess at the material."

"Anyway . . ." Bolan prompted.

"Oh. He had blond hair, blue eyes. Easy, relaxed, laughed quite a bit, but with . . . well, I guess with dignity, or reserve. Nothing at all like the other men. But he was in charge; that much was clear. His name was never mentioned. They all addressed him as 'sir.' They sirred everything they said to him.

He was . . . I would say . . . cultured. And obviously well educated, very self-assured."

"Talked something like this," Bolan suggested, affecting a refined New England accent. "Harvard College, you know, class of Fifty-nine."

"That's him," she agreed quickly. "Sort of like the Kennedys. You know who he is, then?"

Bolan growled, "One of the Talifero brothers. Probably Mike. Has an identical twin. A pair of rattlers, I'll tell you that."

"Yes, I . . . felt that about him. Even though he treated me very nice. Respectful."

"What else?"

"They talked for several minutes, inside the camper, but I couldn't catch much of it. Except that I was to be taken into Trenton. For some . . . I don't know for what. But they kept looking at me and grinning. Made my skin crawl. And they'd decided that the blond man would take Bruno with him, wherever he was going. I don't know why, but I . . . assumed that it would be to somewhere nearby. Don't know how I got that impression, but . . ."

"Think about it," Bolan suggested. "It could be important."

She replied, "Okay. But it's just ahead now. On the left. That service station."

They were arriving at a crossroad.

This was the place where the kidnap convoy from the Tassily farm had rendezvoused with Mike Talifero and his head party.

The spot being indicated by Sara was a small combination grocery and service station. It was closed.

Bolan pulled in to there and immediately consulted

the sectional map that had come with the vehicle.

That spot was marked on the map—circled.

Something else was marked, also, something which he had briefly wondered about and then dismissed as having no consequence that other time he'd studied that same map.

Someone had penciled in a dotted line from this junction to the one where Bolan had paused so briefly about twenty dead men ago—that empty trailer park from where he had telephoned Leo Turrin.

Of course!

So why hadn't he. . . ?

He asked the girl, in a very flat voice, "Which way did they go from here?"

"Straight ahead, the way we just came in."

He hit that road with the transmission screaming into an over-demand response, catching Sara entirely off-guard and causing her to lunge about in the seat and clutch at him for support.

"Wow, you come to quick decisions," she commented when they'd leveled out. "What hit you?"

"A trailer park," he replied tightly.

"That's it!" she cried.

"That's what?"

"It's where I got my . . . The blond man said they would be *at the camp!*"

It was odd, Bolan was thinking, how things had a way of coming together.

It was such a small damn world, and he had to wonder if—via some dimension which the sense perceptions of man had not yet pierced—it was not far smaller than anyone could imagine.

It seemed remarkable to his mind that Bruno

Tassily had known Mack Bolan in Vietnam—however briefly. That, moreover, Bruno had worked for nearly a year at the elbow of Dr. Jim Brantzen; that Brantzen himself had been the first sacrificial victim to the Executioner home-front crusades; and that . . . Hell, there was so much of "coincidence" in the lives of men, sometimes a guy simply had to wonder how much of it was *truly* coincidence.

Bruno had gone to Vietnam to save lives, Bolan to take them.

Bruno's war had never started; Bolan's had never ended.

Bruno had come home from Vietnam to die, Bolan to "live" more vigorously than ever before—Bruno as a man philosophically bankrupt, Bolan just now coming into an understanding of himself and his world.

And then, from Bolan's near-death arose Bruno's new awareness of some of the values of life.

The guy had pulled him out of a half-filled creek, sodden, bleeding to death, with a wound one shade lighter than gangrenous. Bruno the conscientious objector had, in effect, resurrected the Executioner, whose only justification for living lay in killing.

Yeah. Paradoxical. And small, a very small and intricately mazed dimension of being, this place called life.

Smaller yet. The resurrected Bolan had been beating it along the withdrawal trail, seeking a neutral zone, almost home free when he decided to pull in to a deserted trailer park to let the trail ahead cool awhile. And it was from there that the Executioner's withdrawal game had changed, because of a telephone call which he hadn't really wanted to make, and because of a fear which had been born in his dreams.

Very small world, yes.

Because the Executioner was at this very moment hotting it back to that very same trailer park, one which had been deserted such a short while earlier, but one that would accommodate a hell of a lot of big camping vans . . . *when they were not out rolling the highways searching for heads.*

An electric little sensation popped from that compartment of mind where men store their most elemental and vestigial thought processes, and it sent an involuntary shiver along Bolan's spine.

He was wondering where this paradoxical circle of cause and effect would find its natural end. The thing that had wrecked Bruno in Vietnam had been his exposure to countless maimed young bodies.

How would Bruno "take" the deliberate maiming of his own body?

Bolan experienced another tremor, and the girl beside him caught it.

"You're very worried about Bruno, aren't you?" she asked in a tiny voice.

No sense denying it. He said, "Sure."

"Me too. Bruno is so . . . sensitive. He has a very low threshold of pain. I have seen him go to bed sick over a stubbed toe."

Bolan's stomach lurched, and his foot found the floor beneath the accelerator.

Perhaps Bruno had dreams, also.

Maybe it was the dreams that had defeated him at 'Nam.

Maybe he'd had premonitions of his own fate.

Latest U.S. Government
tests of all cigarettes
show True is
lower in both
tar and nicotine
than 98% of all other
cigarettes sold.

Think about it.
Shouldn't your next cigarette be True?

Regular: 12 mg. "tar", 0.8 mg. nicotine,
Menthol: 12 mg. "tar", 0.7 mg. nicotine, av. per cigarette, FTC Report Aug. '72.

Latest U.S. Government
tests of all menthol
cigarettes show
True is lower
in both tar and
nicotine than 98% of
all other menthols sold.

Think about it.
Shouldn't your next cigarette be True?

Warning: The Surgeon General Has Determined
That Cigarette Smoking Is Dangerous to Your Health.

© Lorillard 1973

12 MOMENT OF TRUTH

He parked the car in a cluster of trees about a hundred yards downrange and told his charge, "I'm going to have to leave you alone for a short time, Sara. You follow my instructions to the letter. Get out of this vehicle and go into the middle of that field out there. Lie down. Don't show your head, and don't make a sound, whatever you may see or hear. Don't let anyone approach you, not anyone."

He gave her two small grenades.

"Even if you knew how to use a pistol, which I'm sure you don't, you're better off with these. No big deal here. You just depress the little gadget here and throw it like a baseball. For you, throw it to the ground, right in front of your target. But not too close to your own position. If I'm not back in five minutes, take off. But not in this vehicle. On foot. Stick to the fields, away from the roads. Get to a telephone and call the cops, then stay put. If I do get back—"

"*If?*" she gasped.

"If I do get back, I'll let you know it's me. I'll call you in a way that only I could. Got that?"

Sara nodded and forced a weak "Yes" through

a very dry throat. She took her grenades, carrying them very delicately, and left.

Bolan watched her fade into the darkness; then he began his own move.

He circled in from the rear, pausing every twenty yards or so to sample the atmosphere for sounds, odors, presences; and when he reached the perimeter of the property, he settled there for a full minute, frozen, reading the place, getting its feel, its vibrations; then he moved on in.

The arrival was somewhat anticlimactic. He had somehow expected to find a congregation there. Instead, he found a lone command van and a single crew wagon parked beside it.

There were no sentries.

The curtains were pulled across the van's windows; dull light seeped through.

It was worse than anticlimactic.

The sports car—and therefore Mike Talifero—was not at *this* "camp."

And what of Bruno?

There was but one way to know for sure.

Bolan sprang the Beretta Belle from her side-leather and affixed the silencer, then followed the shadows to that camper door. He tried it, found it locked, rattled the catch, and rapped lightly with the Beretta, calling out as he did so in a convincing New England accent, "Come on, what is this, you all tucked in for the night?"

A drapery moved at the big window, and a blunt face appeared there, squinting out through the darkness.

Bolan stayed with the shadows as he delivered a Talifero laugh and again called, "Going to keep me waiting out here all night, boys? In this no-man's-land?"

The drapery fell back into place, and he heard a hasty rustling inside; then the door cracked open and a guy inside was apologizing, "Sorry, sir, we just—"

Bolan never did learn what "we just" were doing. He exploded through that doorway at that instant, and the guy fell away from there with nine-millimeter whistler up his nose.

Another guy who had been hastily mopping spilled beer from a table just inside hastily released the whole can and nearly turned himself inside-out trying to find a path to his hardware. Another whispering *phu-ut* from the Belle opened an inside-out pathway right between his eyebrows—and there was something a bit messier than beer to mar that gleaming table now.

No one was left in sight or sound.

But then he heard a guy cough from someplace down the aisle, and a testy voice called out, "What the hell're you guys doing out there? Stop the grab-assing around!"

Bolan stepped down to there and snapped open a folding door.

It was the john, and a guy was seated there, pants at half-mast, reading a funny book.

"Hey, what . . . Jesus!" The reaction to the intrusion began as an angry snarl and finished in fading resignation.

The Belle's silencer was making a warm impression on the guy's forehead.

He followed Bolan's eyes up and out of there,

pussyfooting along, with his pants and drawers hobbling him.

Bolan had never met this guy, but he'd seen his mug shots here and there. He was Jack "Scales" Scalisi, up-and-coming muscleman from the Jersey City docks, suspected of complicity in several "unsolved" murders during the current intrigue up there; three arrests, no indictments.

It was rumored, in the tighter circles, that Scalisi was actually a Taliferi, a gestapo super-goon doing a bit of secret-policing for the New York headshed.

Bolan needed no rumors. He knew that Scalisi was one of Mike Talifero's interrogation specialists.

He removed a pistol from the guy's shoulder harness and showed him where to sit. "Get your cock in hand, Scales, and tell it good-bye," he suggested in that graveyard voice.

This was language which a turkey-maker could understand better than anybody. Scalisi's face turned gray. His eyes fled the cold fury confronting him there, to dwell briefly on the two bloodied corpses now decorating his living room. The mouth wobbled, and the voice was dry and cracked when he finally found it. "Jesus, mister, I . . . What can I do? I don't want this. Do you?"

Under more relaxed circumstances, Bolan would have thought that very funny.

The voiced was pitched straight from hell, though, as he replied, "What the hell would I do with it, Scales?"

"No, I don't . . . I didn't . . . I mean, look, sir, I don't even know you. I got no beef with you."

Just a poor sweet guy, fallen in with the wrong friends, no doubt. Bolan asked him, "So what are you doing out here running around the hell grounds?"

Scalisi spread his hands and bunched up his shoulders to indicate his status as a poor victim of harsh circumstances. "Well, I . . . hell, a guy makes a living. Right, sir?"

"Wrong, sir," said the voice from hell. "What you're doing, Scales, a guy makes a dying."

"Well, shit, let's talk it over!" Scalisi squawked. "Let's figure something out!"

"*You* figure something out, Scales."

The guy still had the comic book in his hand.

He stared at it for a moment with glazed eyes, then told the big cold bastard who was standing over him, "I don't blame you for being sore. I'd be sore too. All these guys all over your ass."

It was easy to see that the turkey-maker was bleeding for the Executioner.

Bolan made it official.

He shot him in the knee.

The kneecap just blew away. Whiteness showed there for an instant; then welling redness bubbled and flowed.

The impact jerked the guy halfway around. He flopped back with shock and disbelief mingling with the beginning awareness of massive pain, both hands instinctively applying pressure to shut off the bleeding.

And he was already beginning to bleat, with only one small installment paid.

This turkey-maker had little stomach for the shit, when it was coming *his* way.

"No more silly bullshit," the iceman told him.

"You start talking turkey right now, maybe I'll let you die quick."

The fear of Talifero and of the consequences of broken *omertà* was stronger, at that point, than the fear of death or pain.

Scalisi's mouth clamped shut, and he gave Bolan a pained go-to-hell look.

Bolan gave him, in return, another disappearing kneecap; and the guy fell apart then and there, at the second installment of his tab.

"Leave me alone!" he screamed. "What are you doing? Whattaya want with me?"

"I want Mike Talifero," Bolan calmly told him. "And a guy named Tassily. I want them both, right now."

Those eyes went wild. Scalisi cried, "Mike is . . ." Then he choked and dropped his eyes and watched his life flowing away from him in spurts and rivulets.

"You get to call the next shot, turkey-maker. Balls? Or elbows? You call it."

"They took the guy to the camp!"

"What camp?"

"Down the road! The hunt club!"

"Make me believe it."

"Jesus, leave me alone! I came down and bought this joint out for the week! Mike didn't like it! He took one look and laughed like hell! Went right down and took over that fuckin' hunt club! They run foxes, I think, down there, but not right now! Down the road there, three or four miles! We're just using this joint as a substation! God's truth, that's it! Now, let's get together, let's—"

The Beretta Belle bought "God's truth"—with a softly whispering mercy round straight between the eyes, and the turkey-maker's mouth was still moving as he died.

His suffering had been minuscule, as viewed through the shredded souls of those who had tasted his own applications of shrieking death.

But the muscles in Bolan's cheek were jerking of their own accord as he trotted back to his vehicle.

This was not his style.

He had always tried to kill clean, as any self-respecting "executioner" should.

Only the unrelenting awareness of Bruno Tassily's plight could have moved Mack Bolan into even this microscopic emulation of the turkey men.

And, of course, Jack "Scales" Scalisi had possessed undoubtedly a much higher threshold to pain than the gentle medic, who would find no mercy, no mercy whatever, not even with God's hallowed truth pouring through his lips.

13 ONE FOR BRUNO

He gathered Sara and related, in a half-dozen well-chosen words, the result of his "probe" into the trailer park. Then, following an impulse of the combat sense, he returned to the park, went inside the van, and found the keys to the crew wagon that was parked beside it.

He checked the gas gauge, then hastily transferred Sara and all his effects to the limousine.

As they swung onto the road aboard their new steed, Sara's eyes were asking him the questions her lips would not, or could not.

He told her, "Bruno could still be okay. I think I know where they have him. Guy said a hunt club, three or four miles down the road."

"Oh!" she cried. "Boots and Bugle!"

His eyes flashed as he snapped back, "You know the place?"

"Well, sure, it's only . . . I used to go there when I was in high school. To parties. I never could . . . those adorable little foxes . . . but they rent the place out for local dos. I've been there many times."

"Could you give me the layout?"

"Well, it's been . . . I guess it's the same. Sure. Let's see, it's—"

"Pencil and paper in the map case," Bolan interrupted. "Lay it all out. The property lines, buildings, interiors—I need approximate dimensions, distances, functions, anything and everything you can recall. And damn quick."

Sara's hands were already busy. As she worked her memory, she worked also her mouth—probably, Bolan guessed, as a release of unrelenting tensions. "You think they're doing . . . something . . . terrible . . . to Bruno. Don't you?"

Brutal truth was often far easier to handle than gentle half-truths. He replied, "Yes, Sara. I'd call it a dead cinch. Unless I can beat them to it. And they've already had. . ."

She took a moment away from artful fingers to dispatch escaped moisture from those deep-pool eyes.

Stolen gazes met in the light from the open map case, and she told the man, "I loved the way you called to me, back there."

He had summonded her from her security drop in the field with an impromptu identification signal. "Let's go, Little Mother. Time to build a universe!"

And she'd come running.

Now he told her, "It's past time to *re*build, Sara. Way past time."

He was referring to her own very personal universe, and she whispered the reply, "Yes, I think I understand."

He wanted to leave her alone, to give her memory cells and her artist's fingers full sway, but she plaintively told him, "Talk to me, Mack. Hold me together. I can't . . . I can't believe that all this is actually happening. I mean, right here. This is home.

It's where I grew up, where Mama and Daddy . . . How could this be happening here?"

She was working as she spoke. He assumed that she could work and listen as well. And maybe she needed some anchor to hang on to.

So he let his own stream of thoughts flow into the open, giving utterance to ideas long held but seldom voiced.

"It's an imperfect world, Sara. Nobody with sane mind ever said any different. I'm a soldier, and not much else, but I . . ."

"Oh, you're much more than that," she said. "Go on, tell me, talk to me."

"One psychopath with a hunting knife, you know, can cow and dominate a hundred gentle people. Indirectly, he can enslave millions. It's been done. Many times. Past, present, and . . . I guess, future. It's that kind of world, Sara. It's our heritage. We have to understand that."

The girl was actually sketching the joint to scale —in that moving vehicle in bad light—even shading in terrain features. And with only about one-half of her mind. The other half asked him, "Are you saying that these . . . men . . . are all psychopaths? I mean, these hoods?"

He said, "Sure they're psychopaths. The hard-core bunch, certainly. The ones who dominate. It takes a psychopath to rule brutal men."

Faintly the girl commented, "Oh."

"How's it going?"

"Fine. Please keep talking."

He sighed and checked the odometer. Another mile or two to go. He slowed, to give Sara more time. If he was heading into what he thought, then he would need—and Bruno would need—everything possible going for him.

"It's why the world is always in such turmoil," he went on, aware now that his voice was a sort of beacon for this girl's floundering sense of reality. "Maybe it takes a soldier to realize it. I think . . . there is a 'conqueror' instinct in the human animal. Guys who seek power over other men often are operating from this instinct. All kinds of guys. All kinds of legitimate pursuits. The stronger *it* is, the more dangerous *they* are. If the guy is a psychopath, then look out. If he also is a guy who has no legitimate avenue to power, then the whole world had better look out."

In a murmuring voice, Sara asked, "How do you know a psychopath when you run into one?"

Bolan replied, "It shows, in many ways. This guy answers to only one idea of morality, that idea which tells him that anything *for* him is good, anything *not* for him has just got to be evil. And he can rationalize all the world's great values to fit that framework of what is *good* for *him.*"

She said, "Selfishness, to a fault."

He said, "To a sickness."

A moment later, Sara told him, "It's almost done."

"It sure is," he replied, sighing.

"No, I . . . meant the layout."

"I know what you meant," he muttered.

"Are you going to leave me alone again?"

"Have to," he said regretfully.

She finished the sketch with a flourish of shading strokes and placed it in his lap. "What if I go crazy and start screaming my head off?" she asked.

"You won't do that."

"No, I . . . suppose I won't."

"You're tougher than that."

"Darned right."

"Women are tougher than men."

"They are?"

"Yes, in many ways. Where it counts."

"Mack. I'm going to tell you this, but I don't want you to think . . . I mean, not to make you feel . . . Mack, I love you. I mean, *love* love. Know what I mean?"

Very quietly he replied, "Yes. Thank you, Sara."

"Thank you," she said in a small voice.

He stopped the car, leaned across her, opened the door, dropped a grenade into each of those cupped little hands, and sent *love* love into an open field in the dead of night without even another's voice for a beacon, and in the shadow of their enemies.

It was a hell of a world.

But the only one they had.

Sara had done her work on a large sheet of tracing paper, the kind used for map overlays. It was a highly skillful piece of work, especially considering the circumstances and the time element involved.

According to Sara's sketch, a narrow lane led from the main road directly into the hunt club. She had indicated chain-link fencing surrounding the entire property, and she'd written "infinity" for the distance to the rear border—meaning, probably, a very deep tract of land.

The road frontage she had estimated as "about two football fields"—about two hundred yards, then.

The access lane went off at dead center, ran to a recessed gateway "about four car lengths" off the road—eighty feet or so—then proceeded on a slightly curving path to the "clubroom," a single-story structure which was "twice as wide as my house and three times as long."

Bolan grinned, despite the tensions of the moment.

Some kind of a gal.

It sat upon a rise of land, this indicated only by shading strokes of the pencil. It could be five feet up, or fifty. Bolan bought it as a small knoll, considering the general topography of this particular area.

The interior of that main building was depicted in exquisite detail. Sara must have remembered it fondly. She'd shown a foyer and a large dining-room/lounge dominating the front, smaller rooms at the rear, marked "Bugle Bar," "LR Gals," "LR Boys," "Powder Room," "Office" respectively, left to right. Bolan read "LR" as "locker room."

Other buildings fanned out from the main structure. The stables, leather shop, various other odds and ends. Fox pens and corrals were also depicted. Trails, running into the interior of the property. A meadow, woods, several streams.

That girl had a photographic mind.

And the mental photograph that she had re-created for the Executioner could become a damned nightmare—for a hard hit.

If the place was actually a "camp," then it would damn sure be a nightmare. There could be . . . possibly a hundred, maybe more, hardmen inside that fence.

What was that message from "William Meyer & Company"?

Street-corner recruiting? A run on weapons?

Yeah. Easily a hundred, if this was a field-headquarters site.

And the joint was eminently defensible—chiefly because an invader would have a tough time pinpointing power pockets. They could have fire teams set up all around that property, patrols along the fences, patrols on *horseback*—why not?—and sentries, sentries everywhere.

It was the way the Taliferi operated. Massive power, scorched-earth capabilities. Sure, even in a field exercise. The guys did not gamble. They highrolled.

But it would mean—unless they'd pulled all of their first-line troops in from all around that region of the country—it had to mean that they were going with a recruited *militia*. Green troops—*street-corner* soldiers who even had to go out and buy their weapons before they could join the party.

And all that "sirring" of Mike Talifero, as reported by Sara.

Sure, it fits. And it gave Bolan his "directions to the front."

This would be no hard hit.

This one would be soft, very soft.

For the big softhearted guy.

A soft probe for Bruno.

14 PURSUIT OF THE FOX

He removed his combat rig and placed it in the luggage compartment with the rest of his arsenal, retaining only the Beretta in shoulder suspension.

Then he donned, over the black suit, the same clothing he'd worn from Philly—Johnny Cavaretta's fancy threads, just the slacks and jacket.

The silk scarf, which he had used earlier to bandage the leg wound, was again dazzling white and glossy—and he had to wonder how Sara had managed that. He draped it around his neck and let it fall casually just inside the lapels of the jacket. With that decorative effect, maybe the blouse of the skinsuit would look like a turtleneck sport shirt.

Cavaretta's clothing did not fit Bolan all that well. Too much in the waist, not enough in the legs. He had to compensate for that by wearing the slacks down around his hips, and it came out about right then.

Cavaretta had been one of the VIP hit men, a Taliferi of high rank. Everyone knew, of course, that he was now gone forever. His head had been borne to Augie Marinello as a stand-in for Bolan's, delivered by the gleeful son of Philly boss Stefano Angeletti—and *that* had taken some engineering—

while Bolan himself prowled around the Angeletti headshed posing as Cavaretta.

Frank the Kid's glee had been short lived, of course, woefully deflated—as reported to Bolan by Leo Turrin.

All of this simply illustrated the interesting fact that few living *mafiosi* possessed a really clear idea of what the Executioner really looked like.

Bolan left few survivors in his wake who could provide any sort of coherent description of the man. Since the face job by Doc Brantzen, early in the wars, there were no official photographs of the blitzing warrior. From an occasional and brief eyeball encounter with the law, here and there, various police artists had rendered composite sketches which bore a resemblance—but only a resemblance—to the man in black.

Of course, as Bolan had learned long ago—as far back as that other war, in 'Nam—most people "see" with a clarity and precision which is nowhere in the class with photographic film.

A truly "photographic mind" was a human rarity.

The human mind, Bolan had discovered, was a paradox of itself—a living dimension of space-time, which also, odd as it may sound, *created* space-time.

More than two thousand years before Einstein, a Greek dude of the old world had observed that, "The world is composed of nothing but atoms and voids. All else is illusion."

And the observation was true, even in this modern age of scientific brilliance. It was, in fact, truer than ever. The deeper the scientists probed into the heart of "matter," the more stark became the reality that the world is indeed composed of little more than "atoms and voids"—with the accent on *voids,* or nothingness—sheer energy, arrested here and there in submicroscopically frozen bits that the brilliant minds labeled "matter."

Put a couple hundred billion of those arrested bits together in a losely packed mass, and maybe you've got an atom. Keep putting billions upon billions of atoms together and maybe you'll come up with something which the human mind can perceive— something to "see" or "touch" or "smell" or "hear."

Sure. Bolan was no science-theoritician, but he could understand such things.

The "mind" becomes aware of what the sense perceptions allow inside; and, conversely, the sense perceptions allow inside—to a large extent—only what the "mind" has already been programmed to recognize. Few men living would even claim to understand what the "mind" actually is.

And who had ever actually "seen" a spring breeze?

You felt a movement of something across your skin, sure. Maybe you saw a motion within the branches of trees or in the blades of grass at your feet, and maybe you picked up an odor perception of blooming things which was carried along in that "breeze."

But all you *saw* were *effects.* You never *saw* that rustling movement of molecules in transit.

And few people ever *saw* Mack Bolan—not enemy people, anyway.

They experienced his *effect.*

They usually *saw* no more than something dark and deadly, moving swiftly like a breeze through the limbs of trees and shaking things up and moving them around and scattering them in its path.

And this, of course, was what they "recognized": the effect, the motion—the frightening, mind-numbing, terrifying vision of death in motion.

During those other moments when Bolan chose to walk among them, he was a careful blending of other familiar perceptions. He was "one of the boys" or "just a delivery guy" or "the telephone guy" or something equally innocuous. Sometimes he was a "boss" image, fearful in its own right, benumbing to some minds, perception-scattering through its imputed power over life and fortunes.

And the mob's own modus operandi contributed to Bolan's success with such masquerades. An organization which is based on fear, secrecy, deception, and brutality has a price to pay for the use of those lower attributes. Bolan collected that payment whenever the time seemed right.

And that time seemed right, once again, at this moment in the shrouding Jersey night.

A crew wagon with only one guy inside pulled casually into the little lane and rolled to a quiet halt a few yards short of the chain suspended across the gateway to the place called Boots and Bugle.

Three men stood there, one on either side and the other at dead center. There was a tension in the air there, an alertness mingled with nervousness.

The middle guy stepped down to stand beside the door on the driver's side of the Cadillac, eyes roving the interior of that vehicle.

The window slid down under silent electric power, and the man in there asked the gate boss,

100

"Do you have a light? Four cigarette lighters in this bomb, you would think that one of them would work."

That voice was collegiate New England, calm, relaxed. The guy was wearing sharp threads, a damned scarf, really, lightly tinted sunglasses—at night, yet.

The gate boss hastily dug into a shirt pocket and handed over a Zippo lighter. Helpfully he said, "Maybe it's a fuse, sir. You want me to check it?"

The "big-time torpedo" lit his cigarette and passed the Zippo back. "No, that's all right," he said, blowing smoke toward the guy in the response. "I'll have one of the boys inside look at it. Is Mike here?"

"He . . . Yes, sir, he came in a little while ago."

"Well, I don't believe it. I have been chasing that guy all over central Jersey."

"You've caught him now, sir," the gate boss assured the Executioner. He chuckled as he passed the sign to the gate crew.

The chain came down.

And the Executioner went in.

So, okay. So far.

He rolled casually along the drive, just Cadillacking along, senses flaring into the lie of that place.

Sentries, yeah.

Here and there he caught the glow of a cigarette out there in that darkness, a cough, a muttered word borne along on the evening breeze.

The encampment, yeah. Field headquarters. Division point.

This was it. This was where the Jersey guns were stacked, awaiting directions to the front.

He passed a dignified, lighted signboard emplaced on golf-green lawn, depicting a young lady on horseback, wearing boots and riding breeches and a bright red jacket, jumping a rock wall; in the foreground, the head of a fox with a malicious smile.

So *who* was the fox?

The whole thing could be a cute game engineered by Mike Talifero, a draw, an invitation which the Executioner could not refuse. The guy might be sitting up there in that clubhouse right now, waiting, a malicious smile on his psychopath face.

Bolan sighed and cruised on.

It was no fox hunt, he reminded himself.

It was a turkey chase.

Even if he wound up, himself, the turkey.

15 INSIDE BOLAN

Mack Bolan had not always been a hellfire guy.

Friends and acquaintances of his earlier years were, without exception, shocked over his identification with murder and violence, the unyielding and unrelenting dedication to war everlasting.

His seventh-grade teacher remembered the clear-eyed youngster vividly, and with fondness. "He was a quiet boy. Very smart, a natural scholar. Never rowdy. Very athletic, though. 'Curious,' I guess, is the best single word to describe him. He was the most curious child I ever had. Everything interested him."

A high-school friend, one of the few who was ever very close to young Bolan, remembered, "Mack was a funny guy. You respected him. And you liked him. He was always out front, leading . . . you know, just a natural leader, never a pusher. But sometimes . . . well, you just felt like he wasn't really there. I don't mean nutty. I mean . . . his body was there, but his mind was somewhere else. Mack was a loner."

Another friend, a girl, told a reporter, "Mack was a boy I always felt secure with. I could say things, and he wouldn't make fun of me about it.

He talked to me sometimes, too, I mean seriously. He told me once that he felt like an observer of life more than a participant."

The essence of these candid portraits of the man was more or less accurate. Bolan was indeed a "loner," though not the hermit type who retreats from the world behind a protective shell of cynicism and distrust.

An "observer," yes, certainly. He had never become overly subjective about this thing called life. Even as a very small child, young Mack was more aware of his environment than of himself. He was an observer, very objectively so, and he generally approved of what he saw. He always had the feeling, during the developing years, that he was standing just apart from the rest of creation, never actually immersed in it but still enjoying it, appreciating it. And yet he could feel so strongly about the problems that he noted there, could sympathize so deeply with those who suffered.

He was not, as the psychologists would say, "ego-motivated." He would undertake independent actions, yes, but seldom out of any desire for personal gratification or reward. He was not "materially ambitious." Positive actions usually came about as a result of some outside stimulus—he was "impulse-activated."

The rest of the personality seemed to close around that potentially destructive fact, providing him with a high sense of personal ethics and an underlying dedication toward positive acts of human excellence.

He had never been what one would term a "religious" person. His army personnel file listed him, in this respect, as "No Preference." But Bolan did have a deep religious sense. Undefined, and only vaguely understood perhaps, but he did possess a somewhat formulated concept of a "universal ethic."

The army psychologist who okayed Bolan for the volunteer penetration-team duty in Vietnam had notated the record thus: "Subject subscribes to universalist concepts, appears to be motivated by transcendent ideals (over and above everyday morality). Subject will command himself."

Bolan had been invited to apply for the army's officer-candidate program. He declined, three times by the record, although he was a career soldier. It appeared that he was one of those persons who shied from official authority; but he was recognized by officers and men alike as a natural leader. Others followed out of genuine respect, not because of the stripes on his sleeve.

He had, from the age of about fourteen, kept a daily journal, in which he recorded passing thoughts, particularly impressing events, rambling ideas. Even the most cursory inspection of those journals would convey to the reader a lasting impression that they had been written by a singularly unique individual.

An entry at the age of seventeen: "I stand at the edge of creation and watch the parade go by from my grandstand seat. So powerful, so beautiful, and so *important*. But where am I? Why do I not march in the parade also?"

When he was twenty, and in the army: "Some people were built to march. Others to watch, and wonder why the others are marching, and to where."

A few hours after his first "kill," in a legitimate war: "He was looking into the sun, and suddenly

I was down there with him, looking into his eyes. I saw the entire universe in there. Then I was back where I belonged, my eye to the scope where it had actually been all the while, and I gave him back to the universe. May his soul forgive mine."

Sergeant Bolan had returned many men "to the universe" while engaged in acts of war and in the service of his country. And, in the midst of that other war, his very personal "homefront war" erupted. His father, his mother, his kid sister lay dead in the home where Mack Bolan was born. He was sent home to bury them and to arrange care for an orphaned minor brother.

And the world had never again been the same—the grandstand seat gone forever, Mack Bolan marching, marching, marching . . . all the way through hell.

The hell-fire guy sent the Cadillac beneath the portico and to a gentle halt just uprange from a gleaming Mercedes.

The building was brightly lighted, but quiet.

Paired-off sentry teams strolled at the edge of light, in all directions about that knoll.

The door captain was looking his way and acting like he wanted to call something over as Bolan stepped from the vehicle, but something else was distracting the guy, from the inside.

He lunged about suddenly and grabbed the glass door, jerked it open, poising on his toes as though about to leap.

Mike Talifero swept out of the building, waving his arms and muttering to himself, a big guy hurrying along behind him.

Bolan leaned back into the Cadillac to avoid any direct encounter; they had met eyeball-to-eyeball on a couple of occasions, and he did not wish to push his luck this time—not with so much riding on it.

He heard the big bodyguard yelling to someone to "Get us an escort!" as the powerful engine of the Mercedes roared to life.

The Talifero vehicle went past him on screeching tires and ignored the driveway circle to swing out across the grass for a direct route to the gate.

There was a scramble of bodies at the far side of the building. Car doors slammed, engines cranked. Then two crew wagons sprang away in the wake of the Mercedes.

Something, evidently, was up.

Mike Talifero seldom lost his cool—or so the story went.

Bolan went on to the door and indignantly told the captain, "Well, that was a hell of a thing. The guy just hops in his chariot and drives away without even a wave. After asking me to meet him here at . . ."

The guy on the door was nervous, edgy. He was giving Bolan a respectful once-over as he replied, "I'm sorry, sir, I guess he got some bad news a few minutes ago. And he has this meeting with someone big."

Bolan gave the guy a "who-the-hell-do-you-think-you're-talking-to?" look and told him, "Well, yes, but he runs out and drives away the second I arrive."

The captain became flustered and said, "Well, no . . . I don't think . . . I mean, he had to meet someone down at the airstrip. I'm sure he's coming right back. Why don't you just go in, sir? The bar's open, you can help yourself, make yourself comfortable. I guess he won't be gone more'n about ten minutes."

The guy was holding the door open for him.

Bolan was still being indignant. "I don't know. I believe I'll just go on back."

"Only about ten minutes, sir, maybe less. Wait, let me get . . ."

The guy would not have asked Bolan who he was if he'd been busting to know. It simply wasn't done. Not in *this* outfit. You either knew, or you acted like you did. He was now halfway through the doorway and trying to catch the eye of another guy inside.

"Will you c'mere!" he called angrily to the inside, then turned back to Bolan with, "Jess will show you the bar, sir. Just make yourself comfortable."

Bolan was allowing himself to be talked into staying. He was grumbling as he stepped through the doorway, "Well, I don't like to be treated this way. You can tell him that for me. My time is important, too. I have a territory to watch, myself."

"Yes, sir, yes, sir, I know, these things happen, don't they? I bet he didn't even see you. He had this bad news, and he was late to meet the plane. You know how these things go sometimes."

A big ugly kid in shirt sleeves with an oversized .38 clipped to his belt was standing there taking it all in. This was Jess. He must have thought he was Jesse James, the way he was wearing that hardware. Maybe it was where he got his name; it worked that way in the mob.

Bolan growled, "Hi, Jess. How are things on Third Avenue?"

The kid was torn between a smile and a frown. Bolan said, "Haven't I seen you around there?"

The door captain was awkwardly off-balance, trying to hold the heavy glass door open and keep a foot inside at the same time. Again he implored the visitor, "Just make yourself comfortable, sir." Then he fled to the more comforting environment outside, leaving the hot potato for Jess to handle.

That one was scratching the back of his neck and thinking about Third Avenue. He told the big-shot visitor, "I operate mostly around the Bronx, sir. But I guess you could have seen me . . ." He was obviously hoping that Bolan *had* seen him, highly flattered by the notice. "I get around quite a bit."

They were walking toward the bar.

Bolan asked him, "What's going on here, Jess? Why did Mike go flying out of here that way?"

"Oh, something went sour."

"I hope not what I'm thinking," Bolan said ominously.

"Hell, I don't know, sir. Are you here about the . . . ?" His head jerked toward the direction of the locker rooms.

Bolan snapped, "I sure am."

"Well . . . I dunno, sir. They weren't in there very long with the guy. I only heard him yell once, and then it didn't sound like . . . well, it sounded like Bible stuff. Something about putting a goat out in th' woods, I don't know. Then just a couple minutes ago Mr. Talifero came busting out yelling that they'd hit the guy too hard, too fast. I don't know—"

Bolan snarled, "You go fix me something cold and strong, Jess, while I see about this. Which door?"

The guy's eyelids were fluttering. "The men's locker room, sir. Second door down."

"Stay clear!" the VIP who'd noticed Jess around Third Avenue commanded, and the kid nodded and strode on to the bar.

The Beretta was in Bolan's right hand and the silencer was threading itself aboard when he hit that door at full stride.

Everything Mack Bolan had ever been and ever wanted to be was concentrated on that terrible point in Jersey, that awful moment at the end of the turkey chase—at the very doorway to hell.

16 INTERDICTED

The room was long, narrow. Lockers and benches lined both sides, leaving a narrow aisleway through the middle. It T-ed off at the rear, becoming much wider. Latrines and showers back there—showers left, the others right.

Three, at least, of Mike Talifero's people were in there.

One was in shirt sleeves, shoulder-rigged, leaning with his back to the wall, near the entrance, his attention riveted to the activities in the rear.

The other two were in the wide area, wearing white rain slickers and rubber boots—white originally, but now splotched and splattered with something else.

In that initial glimpse, only one of these was in clear view. He was standing back at about the middle of the area, hands on slickered hips, watching whatever the other guy was doing.

The other one was only now and then visible, moving in and out of sight as he busied himself with something back there in the hidden zone.

A human arm, complete from elbow to fingertips, lay on the floor between the two.

A scene straight off hell's front porch, sure, with

all the usual trimmings of odors and electric tension which moved the small hairs on observing flesh; but something very vital to this scene was missing— a loss that only accentuated the bizarre and unreal and terribly inhuman quality of the moment. *Sound* was missing, as though it had fled before something too terrible to be contemplated through human ears.

Yeah, and it was somehow worse, in this silence.

A human being was being taken apart back there, without benefit of anesthesia—quite the contrary, with every technique at human disposal geared to the positive lack of such relief, and without a murmur from the victim.

The guy at the door straightened quickly at Bolan's entrance but gave him only partial attention as he growled, "Ay, this's no damn sideshow. You ain't allowed in here."

The Beretta was at Bolan's side, partially concealed behind his leg. "Mike sent me," he told the guy. "What's the problem?"

"Shit, you tell me," the doorman replied in hushed tones. "It's spooky. The goddamn guy just sits there smiling at them, no matter what they do. Sal is about ready to walk on the ceiling back there, and I don't blame 'im."

Bolan quickly and quietly put the Beretta away. Something was off-key. But what the hell . . . ?

"That's why, then," he said.

"Why what?"

"Why Mike said to scrub it. And I didn't get it. You know."

The doorman shivered and said, "Yeah. I know."

"Go back and tell Sal I said to clean the guy up. I have to take him out of here."

The guard gave Bolan a guardedly piercing look and said, "Now *I* don't get it."

Bolan shrugged. "Ours is not to reason why, ours is but to . . ." He showed the guy a twisted grin and again shrugged his shoulders. "Go get him."

"Not me, I'm not going back there. I just ate."

"Okay. Go out and tell Jess to move my car down in front of the door."

"What are you doing? I mean, what . . . ?"

"I got the bad straw. I get to dump the guy on Bolan's doorstep."

The hardman smiled sympathetically and commented, "Wherever that is, eh?"

Bolan's insides were yelling at the guy to *move it, move it,* but he held onto the grin and quietly urged him along. "We know about where. But we better have this guy out of here before Mike gets back."

The doorman nodded, gave Bolan a final pitying look, and hurried out of there.

The apprentice turkey-maker had become aware of Bolan's presence. He watched the door guard hurry outside before he took a couple of steps up the aisleway toward Bolan to call up, "God, sir, he's still . . ." The guy did a double-take then, and quickly recovered. "Oh, I'm sorry. I thought you was—"

"He sent me," Bolan said, as he walked down there.

The guy was apologizing. "I never saw nothing like this before. This is the damnedest . . . I've worked with Sal before, sir. This ain't his fault. I'm telling you, there's something queer about this turkey."

The pot calling the kettle . . .

Two large suitcases were opened along that back wall.

Turkey kits.

A miscellany of clever tools, gadgets, devices— the sort of stuff you could pick up at any respectable hardware store. Hacksaws, a blowtorch, several different sizes of cutting pliers, other odds and ends of cutting and drilling tools.

A couple of heavy meat cleavers. Power tools, even. A sander and grinder. A jigsaw . . . for trimming nails? Several small electrical devices, even something that looked like a miniature dentist's drill.

A cattle prod.

Medical stuff. A stethoscope. Hypodermic syringes, complete with carefully racked supplies. Rubber tourniquets, many, of varied sizes.

Some kind of black goop in a gallon can, tarry-looking.

They had brought in a swivel chair from somewhere and backed it into the shower area. A heavy-duty extension socket was strung from a wall outlet and a floodlight suspended from a shower head, to give the ghouls their necessary visibility.

A tape recorder sat upon an appropriated bench, the mike suspended from overhead with the extension light.

And, yeah, this place was hell's front stoop.

Bolan could not see the man in the chair.

The other one—Sal, no doubt—was an elephant of a guy. He was standing on the blood-slicked shower-room floor in a white rubber slicker and probably sweating like hell inside it while another man's blood sweated like hell all over the outside of it.

Sal was grunting and breathing hard as he labored over the thing in the chair . . . and, yes, something was definitely out of focus here.

Bolan steeled himself to stoop down and pick the severed arm from the floor. It was cold already. He handed it to the apprentice and told him, "Wrap it up; we're taking it with us."

The guy's eyes goggled and he said, "What?" But he accepted the grisly object and grabbed for a towel.

Loudly Bolan called, "Sal! Come here!"

The fat man turned around to send a hard stare out of there; then he sighed and waddled forward.

Bolan still could not see the thing in the chair.

The fat man declared, "If I'm not left alone, how am I ever to complete my task?"

He spoke from educated years, and Bolan had to wonder, but very briefly, what had brought the man to this place, this time, this circumstance.

But only very briefly.

"You're not completing it," he coldly advised the turkey man. "Mike says we scrub it. We have other ideas now. Patch 'im up, clean 'im up, we're taking him out of here."

The guy seemed prepared to argue his case. "That isn't fair. There are all manner of ways to get around these things. It's just a question of time. I feel that I must protest—"

"Okay, Doc," Bolan interrupted, guessing at antecedents and probably scoring, "you take your protest to the college of surgeons, eh. But right now you make that guy ready to travel. And don't give me any more shit about it."

The turkey man sighed and turned toward his tool kits.

And then Bolan saw Bruno.

And he shivered and ground his jaws and bit his tongue to keep himself cool.

Bruno was nude and strapped into the swivel chair with a broad leather belt encircling the torso.

Ankles were adhesive-taped to the base of the chair, one wrist likewise to the chair arm. The other wrist, Bolan had just handed over to Sal's apprentice. Near the stump of the remainder, a heavy rubber tourniquet was biting deeply into the flesh, and black goop was caked over the raw opening, which, even so, continued seeping red

Horrible, twisting things had been done to the thigh-hip area, great discolored patches of broken flesh attesting to that. Other atrocities had been committed upon the torso and smeared with the black goop.

The eyes were brimming with fresh thin blood, brought there probably by the fact that all the hair just above and about the eyes had been viciously uprooted, probably with blunt-nosed pliers.

Blood was oozing from both corners of Bruno's mouth, and his chin looked as though it had been singed.

But, yeah, the big softhearted guy who'd lost it all in the surgical tents of Vietnam was sitting there with a beatific smile shining through it all.

A-maze-ing, yeah.

Bolan growled, "Hurry it up! I have to get this guy

116

out of here before Mike gets back. And you both better hope I do."

And he was not kidding about either statement.

Sal was grunting and sighing and pulling things from the medical bag.

"It ain't our fault!" the apprentice whined. "He started right off like that. Well, almost. For about ten minutes he sat there and groaned and gritted his teeth. Then with the first big hit he just flipped out. Started yelling Bible stuff at us. Ever since, he's been just like that. We didn't hardly get started, even."

"He was quoting from Leviticus," the fat man informed Bolan, looking around at him with a resigned smile. "I trust that you will find it in the sixteenth chapter, unless my memory has fogged completely. 'But the goat, on which the lot fell to be the *scapegoat*, shall be presented *alive* before the Lord, to make an atonement with him, and to let him go for a scapegoat into the wilderness.' So you see . . ." Sal spread his arms and shrugged, then waddled over to the "scapegoat."

Bolan muttered, "Yeah, I guess I do."

He sure did.

He saw that something or someone with more authority than the turkey-makers and Bolan combined had interdicted that planned fragmentation of a soul.

"It's a form of autohypnosis," the fat man was explaining. "Imposes what amounts to neural blocks across the sensation centers of the central nervous system. There are ways to overcome this, if I had been given the time. It is quite simply autohypnosis,

117

despite the superstitious shivering of my young friend here."

Yeah, okay, Doc, Bolan was thinking. Call it whatever you like. But the simple truth was that Bruno had snockered them all. Maybe the guy had known what he was about all the while, from the moment he dragged a half-dead hell-fire guy out of blood creek.

One thing was fairly obvious. Whatever Bruno had lost at Vietnam, he'd evidently made a shortcut back through the maze and found it again in this most unlikely outpost of hell.

The turkey-maker was telling him, "All right, my grim friend, your man is as ready to travel as he'll ever be."

"Carry him out to the car," Bolan commanded. "It's parked at the front door."

The turkey man gave Bolan a go-to-hell look, but they took Bruno out, and Bolan followed, carrying the severed arm wrapped in a towel.

Jess was standing in the dining room with a tall frosted glass in his hand, looking as dumb as he was.

Bolan said, "Watch your swinger, Jess," and went on past.

The guy who had been guarding the door to the turkey chamber was now walking quickly ahead of the little procession, hurrying to let them out.

He called outside to the door captain, "Open, mister . . . his door, Tank. The back door. We're bringing the meat out."

Bolan told the guy as he swept past, "Stay hard, man."

"Thanks, I will. You too."

118

The turkey man and his helper put Bruno on the rear deck of the crew wagon and apparently intended to leave him there, draped across the hump there. "Put 'im in the seat, damnit!" Bolan yelled.

They did so; then Bolan shoved the fat man away and growled, "Beat it!"

"I am blameless," he said, as he huffed away.

"The hell you are, guy," Bolan told that retreating back.

He produced a small manila envelope from an inside pocket and handed it to the door captain. "Give this to Mike the instant he gets back," he instructed. "Tell him I have everything in hand."

"Yes, sir, okay, I'll sure tell 'im, sir."

Most of them seemed to be relieved over the departure of both the VIP and the "meat."

Bolan had to reflect again that many of these men probably hated the turkey-makers almost as much as did Bolan himself. So why did they . . . ? What price some men were willing to pay for . . . for what? Was *this* . . . life?

He got behind the wheel and shook the dust of that place from his feet.

The chain was down and awaiting his exit when he reached the gate. He went on through with a curt wave, and powered on out to the roadway, ran quick and silent for a thousand or so yards, then pulled off the road and leaned over the seat.

"Bruno! Can you hear me? It's Bolan. Are you there?"

Very slowly that abused head turned, and the blood-rimmed eyes stared at him without seeing. Seeing *something*, yeah, but nothing of *this* world.

The smile was still there.

He gave a rattling sigh, the eyes went glazed, and Bruno very quietly departed.

Bolan knew it, without even touching the guy or chasing a pulse.

He resettled himself behind the wheel, shook away the emotions that were clutching at him and threatening to overcome, and he went on to pick up Sara.

She responded immediately to his signal, and when she came running up, he quickly told her, "Get in and don't look behind you, Sara. Look at me, *at me*."

But she was already getting in, and already her gaze had been drawn magnetically to what was in the rear, so visible in the illumination automatically provided by the interior lights; and she came unglued halfway into the vehicle, that tender jaw dropping in a grotesque scream-without-sound, horrified eyes locked onto that which was there.

Bolan grabbed her and pulled her on in, and held her close against him as he put vital numbers between them and that insane hardsite back there, and she shivered and groaned against him, choking on her own spittle as she fought the very strong need to scream her head off.

Some miles and some roads farther on, Bolan pulled over and stopped the car and took her in his arms to soothe her, and he told her, "That thing back there is not your brother, Sara. It is an illusion left behind by something that doesn't need it any longer. Don't worry. Bruno is okay. He died living . . . in heaven."

Yes.

But some other dudes were *not* okay, and Bolan

meant to see that they died living in hell, where they belonged.

The manila packet he'd left for Mike Talifero contained nothing but a marksman's medal.

Mike would know what it meant.

The Executioner would be returning to Boots and Bugle.

17 FREE AND CLEAR

The night had become time-worn. Bolan and the girl had found another, final, opportunity for the trading of words, ideas, and mutual comforts—a poor substitute, Bolan averred, for life itself—and now they had arrived at a specially arranged rendezvous with a private ambulance from Trenton.

He parked the crew wagon across the rear door of the ambulance. Two white-jacketed attendants hurried out—well cued on their mission, what to expect, how to handle it.

Bolan stepped from the Cadillac and pulled the girl out on his side.

An attendant gazed at him for a second over the hood of the vehicle and remarked, "So you're the guy."

"Just one of them", Bolan replied.

"Sure. I meant . . . I never expected to see you. Not living and breathing, that is."

Bolan smiled tightly and assured the guy, "I'm doing both. Take good care of my friend, eh?"

"You know it. Uh, good luck. You know."

"I know," Bolan replied quietly. He pulled Sara aside and told her, "We keep saying good-bye. Let's say hello for a change."

"Mack, I . . . I'm not trying to stake a claim but . . . if you're ever hurt and bleeding again . . . well, you know the place."

He said, "Sure." Then: "Sara. The hundred thousand I left with Bruno. I'm sure he stashed it somewhere inside the house. It's free money, Sara. Belongs to nobody, and all the blood has been purged from it. I don't need it. I pick it up as I do. Use it. Hear? Use it."

She dropped her eyes and replied, "I . . . I don't . . ."

"Think of it as insurance money if you'd like, or as a reparation of war. It was the mob's money. I can't think of a better—"

All in a rush she protested, "Mack, there are so many important things to talk about, let's not talk about that."

He said, "Yes, but I've brought nothing but hell into your life, Sara. I'd like—"

"You've brought *life,* where before there wasn't any. Bruno would agree with that. I know he would. He'd been a . . . a zombie ever since . . ."

He smiled solemnly and said, "Okay. Let's leave it there."

The guys had Bruno on a stretcher, and covered, and were carrying him to the ambulance. Even these hardened pros were wearing sick faces.

Bolan told the girl, "It's time."

The guy called over, "You ride up front with us, miss."

She replied, "Thank you. But I think I . . . I'd rather have the time to say good-bye to my brother."

Bolan gently suggested, "Instead, tell him hello, Sara."

"Yes, I . . . guess that would be more appropriate, wouldn't it."

He said, "I guess so."

The guy was holding the rear door for her.

She climbed inside, then turned back for a final look. "Good-bye, Mr. Bolan," she said in a trembly voice. "Stay hard, you hear?"

He smiled, solemnly, regretfully, and he replied, "Thanks, little mother. You too."

The door closed, and a moment later another precious segment of Mack Bolan's life was pulling away from him.

Bruno Tassily and his sister, Sara, were now, however—each in their own way—in the very best of hands.

Those two white-jacketed "attendants" were actually United States federal marshals, on volunteer "quiet duty."

They would see that Sara had nothing further to worry about from the fiends of Jersey.

And now Bolan was free.

Free of responsibility, of obligation to anyone but himself, in this still very deadly jungle called Jersey.

Not, however, free to run.

Mack Bolan had run his last yard across Jersey soil.

One more brief appointment, a few miles along this road, with one Leo Turrin. And then, yes, Mack Bolan was going to show the Jersey guns what one free man could do, when he really wanted to.

He was going to show them with a smash right up their middle.

The Executioner was now free to make war.

And let the universe tremble where it would.

"It's a mistake, Sarge."

"Is it?"

"You know it. You stand to lose everything. While gaining nothing."

"It's not a game of gain and lose, Leo."

"Call it what you want, but it's nutty. Mike Talifero has gone completely crazy. With his own hand he shot four boys right between the eyes for letting you waltz in there and take over that way."

"So we're both crazy. That defines the game, doesn't it?"

"There's nothing I can say to change your mind, is there?"

"Not a thing, Leo."

"Damnit, he already had a hundred guns on that place. Now he's calling them all in, from all over Jersey."

"Fine. I like them in bunches. They get in each other's way. Is Augie still there?"

"So far as I can determine, yes. That's one reason Mike had such a violent reaction. You made an ass of him in the presence of his lord and master."

"Did you come down in Augie's plane?"

"Hell no. I came under my other hat. Augie was already here when you called."

"So that was him."

"Who, what?"

"Mike had gone to an airstrip to meet 'someone big' while I was there."

"Okay, yeah. That would be the little private field three miles south of the hardsite."

"Who owns that joint, Leo? The hardsite, Boots and Bugle."

"Some local. No connection. But he knows the

color of the money he's getting. He has rented to them before."

"Okay. Just stay clear, Leo. Go back the other way."

"Sure. I'll be in Trenton. Hal, too."

"You give me two hours, damnit. Two hours!"

"I'd rather not give you two minutes. You know that. And if Hal—"

"Okay, let's lay it flat. I'm collecting a debt. Tell him I said that. I'm collecting from him."

Turrin shifted about in obvious discomfort. "He knows that, Mack."

"Okay. I don't like it this way either, Leo. Nothing asked, nothing expected, that's the best way. But this time it's special. No writs or clouted courts for those guys, not this time. I've got to flatten that joint."

Turrin sighed. "For the sake of a dead man."

"For the sake of men not yet dead," Bolan icily corrected him.

"Sure, I get you."

"And for my own sake."

"I get that, too." Turrin was smiling his solemn smile. "So give 'em one for me, Sarge."

They each smiled that special smile of two men who thoroughly know each other, and they shook hands, and then Mack Bolan returned to the wars, free and clear, with all goals clearly defined.

18 TALIFERI

All of the crew bosses were assembled in the dining room at Boots and Bugle.

Each of these was a full-time officer in the Taliferi. Every man in the Taliferi was an officer, a rank-holder. These were the elite of the outfit, of all the outfits. There were no "button men" or "street soldiers" in the national police force of the mob.

Their allegiance was claimed by no one Mafia family, though they came, in their origins, from all of them. Now they served the *idea,* the *thing* itself, La Cosa Nostra, that bodiless yet terribly effective alliance for larceny which held all the Mafia families together *as one.* And which, in turn, held together *as one* all the organized-crime outfits on the American continent.

The Taliferi were, to the dark world, what the FBI represented to the fifty United States. But that is a poor comparison. Put the FBI under the total control of a despotic President and his cabinet, answering to none other, and the comparison would be more realistic.

The identical-twin brothers, Pat and Mike Talifero, between themselves technically constituted the entire Taliferi. They were the Commissione's men, and the Commissione comprised the ruling heads of the individual Mafia families. Pat and Mike served this body, as their hard arm, their "voice of authority."

Pat or Mike could hit a *capo*, it was said, on their own authority, for specified high crimes against *the thing*, only. But it was said that the two were empowered to act in such matters without prior approval of the ruling council (each of whom was a *capo*) if it could later be shown (to the satisfaction of the surviving *capi*) that their action was justified.

This is a terrible power to be placed in the hands of any human being, especially when it was being placed there by the persons who would be most directly affected by the use of that power.

The story was probably true, nevertheless. The Taliferi had done that very thing on two separate occasions during the Bolan wars; that is, executed one of their own bosses, on their own say-so.

And this is perhaps the best illustration of the incredible machinations of the world of the Mafia. A world peopled by violent and greedy men, living an ethic which Bolan characterized as "psychopathic," so fearful and distrustful of one another that they authorized and erected a personal "doomsday device" to ensure fealty to one another.

This is tantamount to the U.S. Supreme Court hiring itself an executioner to assassinate on the spot any of its members suspected of misconduct.

It was not a world of reasonable men, this world of the Mafia.

Therefore, the Talifero brothers were, it seemed,

a necessary ingredient of any practical "alliance" of competitive families.

And they did compete. The primary purpose of the alliance was to arbitrate the inevitable disputes arising from the division of criminal spoils and, of course, to put forth a united front to guard against encroachment by other ambitious organizations. La Commissione was at once a Board of Trade, a House of Representatives, a Supreme Court, a Department of State, a Labor Department, and a Department of Defense.

And the Taliferi were their teeth.

Long ago the brothers had begun delegating their authority to sharp up-and-coming youngsters in the various families. Like any government function, the bureaucratic spread grew as the job grew, and the job grew as the bureaucracy flourished and sought new tasks to justify its existence.

For some time now the Taliferi had been a national gestapo, replacing the old Murder, Inc. headshed of the early years, wielding a power like no "family" had ever dreamed of.

But it was, in essence, a family in its own right.

It was a family of "elite" cutthroats, many of them fairly well educated and polished, but cutthroats nevertheless.

And the family of the elite was in session at the Boots and Bugle on this fated night in New Jersey.

Their co-*capo*, Mike Talifero, was presiding.

Brother Pat was still recuperating from grievous and near-fatal wounds received in the Executioner's Vegas rumble.

Greatfather Augie Marinello, reputed "boss of all the bosses"—which simply meant that he was the most influential and feared member of La Commissione—was also present, though almost in a *capo emeritus* status.

Little actual information is recorded on the Talifero brothers. That they were brothers was obvious—they were identical twins—but even the name itself was suspect. Perhaps it is significant that it is a blending of two Italian words: *tale* meaning "such" and *ferro,* "iron."

Mike was thought to be about forty years old, certainly no more than that. He was of Sicilian origin, and rumors had him a tenth-generation *mafioso.* He had originally come into the outfit, it appears, under the sponsorship of Marinello—at that time an underboss in the New York family which he now ruled.

There had been a time when the Talifero brothers rarely smiled. Since Miami, though, and that terribly dismal first encounter with Mack Bolan's mind-blowing brand of blitzing warfare, the brothers had been given to smiling and laughing it up quite a bit. Those closest to them knew, too well, that Pat and Mike were in their most deadly moods when they were smiling and laughing it up.

Tonight Mike was smiling a lot and treating the boys to quite a few laughs as he briefed them on the plan for the night.

Twelve tried-and-true men were in his congregation, the elite of all the elite, and they had been brought to Jersey specifically to collect Mack Bolan's hated head.

Each of those present was, at the moment, bossing a crew of ten to fifteen "free-lance" guns—small-time hoods scooped from the streets of Manhattan and north Jersey and pressed into this emergency service. These "soldiers" were not members of the brotherhood. Some were blacks, some were white Anglos, some were Puerto Rican and Irish Catholic and Jewish and whatever else could be bought by the week for the business end of a gun.

There is no national origin to crime.

It comes in every form and guise. The 99.9 percent of good people in the Italian-American community cannot be held to blame if some of their number seem to have a genius for organization and if some of those found a way to make crime pay.

But this *was* a Mafia party, let none wonder about it; the Mafia *does* exist, and it appeared to be alive and well in New Jersey on that night of nights at the makeshift hardsite at Boots and Bugle.

It was a council of war.

And the Taliferi were ready and waiting for a certain son-of-a-bitch to show his tail around that place once more, just once more on that hellish night of all nights in the life of smiling Mike Talifero.

19 APOLOGIA

He made a soft run to the rear of the property, circling in across adjacent farmlands on a cross-country approach, running dark and quiet until finally reaching a stand of trees which marked the property lines.

It was shortly past midnight.

Incredibly, twenty-four short hours earlier he had lain sleeping in the loft of the Tassily brooder house, recuperating in a forced détente. He had lived, it seemed, several lifetimes since then.

Already in Jersey he had killed more men than even a dedicated executioner cared to contemplate. But Mack Bolan did not count the dead, not the *enemy* dead. Body counts had meaning only as applied to the living ones.

And that was the purpose of this initial mission.

He had to go in there and count them, locate them, classify them, assess their strong and weak points, establish an angle of attack, determine objectives . . . and figure out a way to get out of there once the battle was ended to his satisfaction.

Mack Bolan was not a wild-ass warrior.

Hell-fire and thunderation were his trademark,

yes, but his blitzers were usually undertaken with cool military preparedness.

He was not anxious to die; willing, perhaps, if that was the way the numbers fell. But he would work those numbers to every possible personal advantage. Victory, for Mack Bolan, was measured not in points of time or as triumphant events; victory in war for the Executioner meant remaining alive to wage war.

He left the crew wagon in the trees and stripped himself to the black suit, forsaking all weapons except stiletto and garrote.

Then he gooped his hands and face and moved out, a fleeting shadow of the darkness, a silent sigh of the night, a mere "observer" at the edge of creation.

Moments later he was inside the enemy compound, moving catlike through the tall grass at the fence line.

When he moved, it was swiftly; when he paused, it was almost cataleptic in its abrupt cessation of all sound and movement.

On a soft penetration, Bolan became to all effects a part of the landscape, *one* with the universe enveloping him, in complete harmony with the nonlife elements.

As the wind rustled through the grasses, so did Bolan.

As shadows leaped with scudding clouds or moving branches, so did Bolan.

And when the universe held still for a moment, so too did Bolan.

The asphalt and concrete boys of the urban jungles were clearly disadvantaged in this game with this child of the universe. Bolan was "at home" here; it was his sort of jungle, and the night was his bosom companion.

So it is no discredit to the street soldiers from Manhattan and Newark, Jersey City, and Brooklyn that the man from thunder moved undetected through their midst, studying their movements and divining their defenses, reading their fears and anxieties, exposing their weaknesses and contemplating their strengths.

He "sectored" them, and made "grid overlays" in the retentive web of his combat consciousness.

He "psyched" them, and made mental combat notes on how best to capitalize on the natural inclinations of this motley army of mercenary ragtags.

Actions under the stress of combat are more often than not purely reactive things, a flexing of the survival instincts along a pathway of strongly conditioned (trained) responses.

The actions before a battle are usually the foretelling of the tale.

Combat—in the organized sense—is a uniquely human pastime, despite the outraged cries from humanitarians down through the ages that combat is bestial, inhuman. It is, literally, intensely human.

The art of combat was perhaps the first art ever devised by the human mind, and the high development of this "art" made man supreme over the other beasts. It is uniquely his accomplishment, even if also his damnation.

The first tools ever developed by the hands of men were very probably tools of combat, and to this day the greatest excellence of technology is usually

134

directed into or produced by this same class of tool-making.

The very intellect of man was fashioned both by and for the grim necessity to do battle, to survive through combat, and many of the most stirring moments of human history were productions of the combat intellect.

To dismiss "soldiers," then, as something less in the human order than artisans and philosophers and prophets is to degrade the very foundations of humanity.

Without the soldiers, the "combat intellectuals," there would be no artisans and philosophers and prophets; nor would the mind of man have ever descended from the trees to survive the brutalities of life on the jungle floor, and on the plains and plateaus of a natural world which knows no natural peace.

There *is* an intellectual excellence inherent in any victory of man over the elements; and man himself, of course, is an "element" of the natural world. Let the "intellectuals" boo and hiss at the military mind as they may, and do—there *is* a human excellence and an intellectual brilliance present in the finely tuned *organized combat sense*. Each boo and hiss sent up from the others has been paid for, made possible by, this older and more refined and superbly excellent exercise of the human intellect . . . and paid in blood.

This does not, of course, mean that combat is necessarily good. At its best, it usually represents the lesser of two evils. But it is, always has been, and—so long as man *is* man—will probably remain necessarily *necessary*.

In any human necessity, we usually find instances of human excellence, high achievement, sincere dedication, genius.

Bolan the warrior was a personification of these very human attributes.

There are those, of course, who follow an innate combative instinct, a raw and untempered yearning for unearned riches and for arrogant power over their fellow humans.

For the gentle folk of the world, then, it is fortunate that men of high human ethics and excellence have applied their energies and intellects to the problems of survival in a brutal world. It is this circumstance, and this alone, which has saved the finer minds from the savages among us.

As Mack Bolan pointed out to Sara Henderson, a lone psychopath with a knife can dominate a hundred gentle people.

By that same token, one finely tuned intellect with a disciplined combat sense can overcome a hundred untrained savages.

Mack Bolan was living proof of that.

It seems a pity, a very human pity, that so many fine minds do shrink from the responsibilities, the everyday dirty and mucky responsibilities of maintaining the world in the face of constant savagery.

And this little detour through the back roads of the World of Bolan is not intended as an apology for the man or his methods.

It is an apology for those who boo and hiss.

20 THE SET

In every sense of the word, the joint was a hardsite. Its defenses had been thoughtfully devised and painstakingly erected, and they were being carefully maintained.

The obvious defense perimeter was an oblong encirclement of the small knoll upon which sat the clubhouse and its outbuildings, the line running about one hundred yards from front and rear, extending one hundred and fifty or so yards to each side.

This was a fire line, with "set" teams of two men each emplaced at intervals of ten yards. These guys were simply chunked out there, entirely visible and with no physical protection whatever, sitting or lying or standing around, talking freely from set to set, trying to while away a long wait in a longer night.

Pistols, mostly. Here and there a shotgun.

This was the dumb line. Bolan had seen them before. So much live meat staked in the jungle to attract the lion. And the poor bastards didn't even know it.

On the rooftops and concealed within the outbuildings were the primary defenses, the "trap sets."

There were marksmen with rifles on those roofs.

Automatic-weapons experts with choppers large and small prowled the shadows of the main building and lurked in the recesses of other buildings.

Undoubtedly, more troops would be found in and around the parking area at the side of the clubhouse, where many vehicles of various types reposed in the quiet wait.

The outer defenses were no more than an early-warning attempt—a combination of solitary set-men scattered widely in no clear pattern and roving patrols of two men each.

Miniature radios and shotguns.

Bolan had counted one hundred and eighteen enemy heads, and he was satisfied that this took care of most of the numbers. There would be others inside the clubhouse, certainly, a "palace-guard" last ditch for the ranking big shots.

Sara's "photographic-mind" sketch of the property had omitted one more or less insignificant detail. Perhaps it was one of those repressions of the psyche which so troubled intelligence-seekers. She had "forgotten" the kennels yard, the place where the hounds were kept, the hounds that chase "adorable little foxes."

It was one of those chain-link affairs with a wire-mesh top, featuring a private run and individual shelter for each dog.

And the dogs were present, about twenty by Bolan's long-distance count—nervous, and pacing, with some primeval sensing of the portents in that night.

If there were horses in the stables, he could find no such evidence. Bolan had thought that clubs such as these probably boarded members' horses, but the question seemed to have no relevance to the night, and he dismissed it.

He knew that it was impossible to account for every conceivable defense that an enemy may have "up the sleeve."

But he was satisfied that he had collected their prime numbers, and this had been the objective of the probe. He knew enough about them now to give himself, at the least, a practical angle of attack, a numbered approach which more than likely could bring him into the destruct zone with most of his firepower intact.

The primary question remaining was: the destruction of whom and which?

That, of course, was one of the variables of warfare. In the final analysis, every act of war was a gamble—a gamble with the universe in which all the odds were concealed, hidden away somewhere in that "universal maze of cause and effect."

The most a guy like Bolan could do would be to introduce the "cause" in his most skillful and persuasive form of argument.

The rest would be up to the court—that Supreme Needs Court of universal law—and the combatants would have to abide by that final "judgment in the wind."

Mack Bolan, in his own mind, was a living instrument of the universe—a sensory extension into that which was—as were, he believed, all living things.

He could only hope that the winds blowing across

central Jersey in this time and circumstance were winds of justice and high purpose.

In any other context, the Executioner was indeed involved in a damn-fool exercise.

21 IN THE WINDS

It was drawing onto two o'clock, and the previously sharp edge of the night was beginning to writhe in anticlimax.

Mike Talifero paced the small office of Boots and Bugle and squeezed his palms together behind his back.

Augie Marinello, the Invisible Second President of the United States, occupied the nearest approximation of a throne available, a luxuriously padded executive chair at the desk.

His two trusted "tagmen" (chief bodyguards) of long standing went right on standing, in his shadow, revolvers nervously exposed through the opened coats of two-hundred-dollar suits.

"Why doesn't he hit?" Talifero muttered, the tone of voice strongly belying the set smile of that face.

Marinello removed a long cigar from his teeth to observe calmly, "The guy comes at his convenience, Mike, not ours. You should've learned that by now."

"I was just talking to rattle my tongue," the gestapo chief said. "I know what the guy is doing."

"There's always the chance he won't come tonight

at all," the *capo* pointed out, for perhaps the twentieth time.

"You're forgetting Boston," Talifero said.

"I'll *never* forget Boston," Marinello assured him.

"The guy goes off his rocker when he finds a turkey. Look at what he did to Freddy, that time in New York. Over a dumb kid he hardly knew. How do you think he feels about *this* one? The guys were battlefield buddies in Vietnam. This guy worked with the surgeon who gave Bolan his new face, out in California."

"I know, I know."

"Well, what do you think this is doing to that guy's guts? He's crazy, I'm telling you, crazy for revenge. He's running around out there somewhere just crazy as hell, trying to come up with a way to hit us. I know that, and you know that, Augie."

"Don't get assy with me, Mike."

"You know I'm not . . ." Talifero halted his pacing and told the big boss, "I'm sorry, Augie. Bear with me through this, huh? This is a hell of a—"

"I know." Marinello's cigar had gone out. He frowned at it, then cast a reproachful glance at the nearest tagman. The guy leaned forward with the ever-present lighter and applied new heat to the five dollars' worth of hand-rolled tobacco leaves. The old man puffed new life into the cigar, then told his fair-haired boy, "You're taking this too personal, Mike. You're going to fool around and stub your toe again. You better back off some."

And that was a hell of a thing to say. Right out in the open, that way. Talifero shot an angry look in the general direction of the bodyguards. It had not been a thing to say to the hardarm of the whole damn world, not with underlings present.

Without looking at the boss, he quietly stated, "I have never stubbed my toe, Augie. You don't run an outfit like this with stubbed toes. You know that. Why are you needling me? At a time like this—"

"This is exactly the time," the old *capo* shot back. "I've been counting the score, Mike—me and some others. It's why I came down, myself, personal. You missed the guy at Miami. You missed him in Vegas —damn near permanently. Your brother is still a vegetable from that. You missed Bolan at Philly. And you've been missing him here in Jersey all week long. You can understand, I know, if we start wondering, Mike, just when you're going to start connecting."

"Well, what a hell of a time to . . ." The famous Talifero smile was absolutely plastered from one ear to the other. In a voice as calm as cold soup he recovered himself and told the boss of bosses, "That's not fair, Augie. I have never before had absolute control over any situation involving that bastard. You know that. I've always been called in to save a losing situation after most of it was lost. This time is different. This time the guy is dancing on *my* strings. I'm going to get that son-of-a-bitch this time, Augie, if I have to go out and do it on my own. I am going to get him alive . . . and I am going to keep him alive for a long, long time."

"That's exactly what's got me worried," Marinello quietly replied. "I think you got too much of your own ass in this thing."

"Then take me off."

"You know I won't do that, Mike. You're the best

there is. I just want to be sure you keep your own ass out of the way. Get the bastard, Mike. Roast his dick off in boiling oil if that's what you gotta do, but *get* 'im first. Any way you can. Forget the fancy horseshit. Just *get the guy!*"

"I fully intend to."

The *capo di tutti capi* arose abruptly from his chair. "And just in case you don't, I'm going back home."

"That could be a wise decision," the gestapo boss said icily. "But not for the reason given."

The two architects of human misery locked gazes, and the little flares deep within the wily old eyes of the man who had built an empire of it from nothing but nerve and determination clearly showed an awareness of and distaste for this other monster of his own creation.

"I made you, Mike," he reminded his hardarm. "I can unmake you just as easy."

"That would be at your pleasure, of course," Talifero replied stiffly, smiling the deadly smile.

"Just don't get any assy ideas, that's all. I put out a memo before I come down here. The council is going to review this whole setup. Just don't try anything assy in the meanwhile."

"That's an ultimatum, isn't it?"

"I'm not sure I know what that means, Mike. You college boys have it all over me in the word department. I'm just telling you to get this Bolan. If you can't get *him,* maybe we're not so sure about the way you might handle other things. You get me, Mike. You know what I'm saying."

"I know, Mr. Marinello. What I don't get is why

you're springing it at a time like this. I need confidence, not a knife at my back."

"You're the boy with all the knives, Mike. We just wanta make sure you know how to use 'em, that's all."

The *capo* swept out, a tagman at front and rear. He picked up another small group who were waiting just outside the office door, and the party from Manhattan moved swiftly toward the main exit.

Mike Talifero appeared in the doorway to call out instructions to his own troops. "Mount a convoy! See that our friends get back to their plane and off the ground safely!"

Marinello halted in mid-stride to throw back a counter-command. "Never mind that. We'll take care of our own selves our own way!"

This was not only an open slap in the face for Mike Talifero. It was also an open statement of mistrust by the boss of bosses in his commander-in-chief of the armed forces.

Mike himself knew that, even if every other man in the building did not.

The Marinello party moved on, and before it had even cleared the building, a Taliferi lieutenant burst in through a side entrance and hastened to the side of his boss.

"Okay, it's started," he announced tensely. "Charlie just stumbled on two of our boys down on the early line, necks broke, dead."

Mike Talifero chuckled and commented, "Well, well."

"You want me to stop Augie?" asked another lieutenant who had been standing by.

"By no means," the hardarm of the world replied quietly. "By no means whatever."

While outside, with a promising wind at his back, the Executioner was about to find his first great windfall of the long night.

22 INTO THE MAZE

Bolan had quietly withdrawn from his soft probe and returned to his temporary war wagon, with hardly a blade of grass disturbed to mark his transit through that enemy territory.

He sprang the arsenal from its storage in the luggage compartment and put together everything he could carry.

He would very probably not be coming back this way again.

In addition to the usual combat rig, he was now burdened with back and chest packs, loaded with the necessities of one-man warfare.

A one-man army had also to double as pack mule, from time to time, and this was clearly one of those times.

The packs featured quick-disengage buckles. He could come out of them in a flash, if necessary.

Fully engaged, he estimated that he was now carrying a load almost equal to own weight. He experimented with the tender leg and found just a bit too much demand imposed there. Regretfully he jettisoned several of the heavier munitions and went on. With all votes counted, he would need his own physical prowess more than a few items of hardware.

He was not traveling the edge of creation on this trip through. He was at the very center of it, and he had to clear a path as he advanced—a trail through a jungle of jumpy amateur warriors whose first loud alarm would mean Bolan's premature exposure, and undoubtedly a quick end to an unhappy night.

The object was to get in close, undetected; to make some sort of setup from where he could send war winging into several quarters at once; to induce confusion and panic, paralysis in the enemy, and, hopefully, full flight on the part of the ragtag street-corner bad guys who'd hired out their guns for a war they knew nothing about.

This would be a sort of victory in itself, but of course, this was not the primary objective of the night.

It was but a means to an end.

The end was Mike Talifero.

He meant to execute that guy, and leave him with a marksman's medal lying atop the wound.

Maybe someday other guys would get the message, deciding that the wages of command in this outfit were too poor for the risks involved.

At that moment, though, Bolan had to admit to himself that his objective of the night was but a forlorn desire, not a true and viable goal of the battle.

He would consider the mission a success if he could simply storm in there and rattle them, scatter them, scare the living hell out of them, and make them wonder why they'd come—destroy their smug pride and wipe that arrogant "lord-of-the-realm" sneer from their faces. And make them think twice the next time around, when another helpless victim of storm-trooper tactics lay at their mercy.

For the moment, he had to *sneak* in, and cover his progress with every wile of silent combat.

And twice during that quiet reentry he shrugged out of his mule packs and slithered in with the sighing wind, to silence quickly and efficiently a potential alarm post.

These two were his only obstacles, and he reached the eastern perimeter of the dumb line with his mission intact and with an angle of attack rather clearly formulated.

And, at that point, he received a bit of assistance from the enemy themselves.

A tri-mount of floodlights was emplaced at the front corner of the clubhouse, angled toward the parking area. These floods were lighted, had been throughout the long wait, and they were the only outside lights in use.

Bolan had pondered the fact on his earlier penetration, deciding finally after much weighing that this was a weak point in the enemy defenses; moreover, one which the enemy also recognized. The vehicles massed there presented a possible point of cover for an invader who might slip through to that point; also, they represented a potential weapon.

If a guy could get in there and spill some gasoline around, he could get one hell of a whomping jazz-bang going with all those exploding gas tanks.

They would not disperse the vehicles—not this outfit. Mack Bolan was not their only enemy. The boys always liked to have good wheels quickly available, should the ever-present threat of the law suddenly materialize.

At the same moment, they could not adequately defend such a motor pool against a determined aggressor—one like Bolan, for instance—so they simply lit it up and dared the bastard to come in.

While admitting that the motor pool jazz-bang would make a nice effect, Bolan had already written it off as too risky without sufficient payoff. He did not accept invitations to combat. He issued his own.

Still, he had seen a way to use the situation.

It was why he had come in at this particular angle to the dumb line. The defense perimeter had been emplaced on the low ground, below the knoll and surrounding it. Looking back toward the clubhouse from this particular point, a guy would be staring straight up into those blinding floods on a direct line of maximum effect.

Bolan himself did not intend to look into those lights.

He did, however, desire to persuade this particular sector of the dumb line to squint up there, if only for a few seconds—long enough to put the pupils of their eyes into sharp contraction and induce a moment or so of night blindness in the defensive line.   It was a simple tactic, sure. But it should work. Well enough for a quiet shadow of the night to slip through that line and head for the high ground. From that moment on, the people behind him would never again see him. Each time they looked his way, they would see nothing but blinding floodlights.

And so it was that Bolan was preparing to breach the dumb line when the excitement up there in the vehicle area provided the distraction he was already planning.

Several men had run from the front of the building to the parking lot and were cranking the engines of three crew wagons.

Bolan was crouching in the grass, a frozen illusion of the night, about twenty yards out and dead center between two of the paired-men sets on the dumb line.

The dumb men had been quietly talking within their own sets until those engines up there fired. Then one of the guys just uprange from Bolan called down to the next set, "Hope they're not bailing out on us, man."

One of the guys down there chuckled nervously and called back, "You got paid in advance, didn't you, man?"

"Sure. But they never mentioned no death benefits."

"Or bail," another snickered.

This entire sector was now staring toward the hill.

Bolan, mule pack and all, made his penetration while a guy farther up the line was exclaiming, "That's that boss from New York!"

"Which one is that? They're all from New York."

"The old man. The big boss . . . What's-his-name."

"Manischewitz," someone offered.

"Naw, that's a wine."

"Same difference."

Bolan had missed none of it, and now he was moving swiftly along the base of the grassy knoll, in smooth golf-green now, swiftly seeking the most favorable spot in which to set up his fire base.

He found it about midway up the hill, amidst the

foundations of the signboard with the daring young lady and the leering fox, the lights of which were now prudently extinguished; and it was the sheerest of coincidences that this spot also provided excellent command of the driveway where it circled off the hilltop and dropped into the straightway toward the main gate.

Bolan had hardly touched down and shrugged away his packs when the first vehicle in the Marinello procession came whining into the descent.

This was a quick-reaction situation—an instant flicker of the instinctive combat sense—and Bolan the warrior did not even question the route that had brought him here. He simply sent an unformed thanks to the powers behind the winds and made a quick selection of weapons.

"*Entrez-vous,* Augie," he sighed as the second vehicle nosed into view.

Step into my *maze,* the spider should have said to the fly.

Yeah, and Bolan could feel that universal wind at his back for sure now.

Augie Marinello, boss of all the bosses, was a much riper plum than Mike and all his Taliferi combined.

The Executioner would make at least one positive statement on this night to top all nights in Jersey.

23 THE HIT

The limousines surged in beneath the driveway portico, and the Marinello party quickly embarked, the boss himself stepping into the sandwich vehicle with his two tagmen sliding in behind him to occupy the rear-facing jump seats in the center.

Another bodyguard leaped into the front beside the driver, and the procession moved out.

The haste was not entirely motivated by a desire to quit that bastion of Taliferi power, though that element was certainly present in the nervous departure.

The *capo di tutti capi* usually moved from point to point in this fashion, quick ins and outs, moving swiftly, with fully crewed escort wagons to front and rear.

In the home stand, Augie used a bulletproof vehicle that he often compared with that used by the President.

This trip was in an ordinary crew wagon, though one equipped with all the animal comforts and conveniences.

The possible presence of Mack Bolan in that particular area also undoubtedly influenced the emotions in this instance, but the conversation of the moment clearly pointed toward that other danger.

"Pardon me if I'm out of line, boss," the chief bodyguard said as he was settling into his seat, "but I don't like the smell of this place."

"Don't worry, me neither," Marinello muttered glumly. "I'll fix that when I get back, you better believe it."

They were facing each other across the rear deck.

Marinello flicked his again-dead cigar with thumb and forefinger. The tagman leaped to light it.

The radio up front crackled with a question. "To the airport, boss?"

The *capo* grabbed a mike from the armrest to reply, "Naw. Go on straight home, the turnpike. Let's not dick around here another minute."

The crew chief in the lead vehicle acknowledged the instructions as the procession picked up speed leaving the turnaround.

"Run close, but not too close," Marinello instructed his own wheelman as they swung into the descent.

The chief bodyguard was wondering about something else. "How 'bout Marty, boss? He'll be sitting down there with the plane all night."

"Call him when we get back. Not until."

"Right, sir, I getcha."

The Marinello vehicle was slowing for the final curve at the base of the hill when the electrifying event occurred.

Something crashed through the rear window directly between the boss and his tagmen and fell to the floorboards with an ominous thud.

The chief bodyguard still held the cigar lighter

154

in his hand. He dropped the lighter and lunged toward his boss in an instinctive defensive reaction; then he yelled, "God, it's a damned . . ." and began scrabbling along the floor with both hands.

Marinello was screaming, "Stop the car, stop!" when the whole wide world turned red before his eyes and his chief bodyguard was suddenly lifted toward the ceiling with a roll of flame beneath him.

The limousine did not take that final curve.

It lurched on in a straight line of travel, bounded across the graveled shoulder and along the bottom edge of the slope for about half a car length, then slowly teetered onto its side and on over into a wheels-up slide to the bottom.

Then it exploded again, this time from the rear, and the last thing to occupy the exploding consciousness of the boss of bosses was a question: Who did it? Who did this awful thing? Was it Mike, or was it Mack?

It was Mack, and he did it with a hand grenade, baseballed into the target with major-league precision, and he did not even take the time to assess the results.

Without consciously realizing that he was counting numbers, he had a flare round loaded and ready to fly, awaiting only the cover of the first explosion to launch it.

With that larger roar came the barely discernible *phut* of the launching which sent that silent streaker into the northern skies beyond the clubhouse.

During that second or two which separated the second explosion within the Marinello vehicle from the opening of that celestial floodlight, a group of hardmen from the front of the clubhouse had dashed

155

over to the edge of the hill to gawk at the spectacle below.

Someone screamed, "That's Mr. Marinello down there! Get down there! You boys get down there and pull 'im out!"

But as that horrified command was being issued, the sizzling white light of the flare popped into brilliance and began settling across those back acres, and someone else yelled, "Twelve o'clock high! Watch the rear! You boys get back there and cover that rear!"

Another excited command blended with that one to direct the men on the rooftops: "Riflemen! Keep alert! Watch your sectors! It's a trick!"

So, okay. Quickly on the tail of that, the riflemen had other problems to ponder. From only God knew where, in all that yelling confusion, something very disconcerting came whizzing out of the darkness on a thin tail of fire. It struck the chimney atop the clubhouse and exploded in a shattering rain of shrapnel and flying chips of brick.

Pandemonium erupted up there, while back at ground level some of the men from the dumb line had surged in from the front perimeter to assist the Marinello people who were frantically trying to pull bodies from that flaming wreckage.

Another grenade dropped into their midst, out of nowhere, and the dumb men raced back to the edge of darkness.

Someone down there yelled, "Well, *fuck* it! I didn't sign up for *this!*"

Another shaky voice seconded that conclusion at about the same moment that the glass front of the clubhouse disintegrated in another shattering explosion.

A Taliferi lieutenant ran halfway down the hillside to shout into the night, "You boys get back here! Where the hell you think you're going?"

Anyone standing close enough and with mind enought left to perceive would have heard the deadly *phu-uut* of a silenced Beretta, and perhaps would have even discerned a slender pencil of flame emanating from the base structure of the club signboard at about the same instant that this same lieutenant sprouted a mushrooming hole in his face and toppled down the hill.

A voice out there in the darkness, a bit fainter now, yelled back, "We ain't going where you're at, man. Not for no five hundred bucks!"

And the battle had hardly begun.

Vehicles were lurching away from the motor pool and taking the scenic cross-country route to the gate, and the surviving Taliferi had given up trying to threaten and cajole the fainthearted troops to remain and give battle.

It was an understandable problem.

There is something particularly jarring to the psyche of even well-trained troops when high explosives begin thundering through the night, when friends and buddies erupt into frothing fountains of blood and die screaming, and especially when even the leadership becomes shaky and disorganized.

Green troops, never exposed to the hellish realities of honest-to-God warfare—nor even to the conditioning courses of the training fields—cannot be expected to stand firm through such an experience.

Bolan knew that. He had been counting on it.

But then something else occurred in the midst of that hell fire which Bolan would wonder about later.

From down around the Marinello wreckage, someone had yelled, "We need an ambulance."

Another voice replied, "Fuck that. Put 'em in your car and haul ass for Trenton."

"He's gonna die! Just lookit his legs! That old man's gonna die!"

"If you don't get moving, we're all gonna die! That fuckin' guy is right over there somewheres. Right under our noses!"

"Wanta try for the cars again? Think we can make it?"

Hearing, Bolan consigned Augie Marinello's aged fate to the needs of the universe. He sent a brief burst of chatter fire around their heels, then called down to them, "Is the old man alive?"

A startled voice came back muffled and about one beat off its numbers. "Yeah, just."

"Okay. I'll give you a white flag. For five seconds. Beat it!"

It was the first "white flag" Bolan had ever given in the heat of a Mafia war. He was to wonder about it later, and decide that it had been a small concession to the nobler instincts of the human animal.

He watched them scamper to the remaining vehicles, bearing their wounded into a hasty load and exit; then he turned back toward the jungle.

Those fleeing vehicles would only serve to deepen the battlefield trauma of those hired by the week.

Let them go, too.

Let all the weak bastards go.

He wanted the lords—the lords of this rotten jungle.

He checked his belt clips and filled in the blank spots with concussion grenades, heavy ones, swung the chatter pistol to the rear, and draped another belt across his shoulders.

Then he picked up the weapon of the night, the M-16/M-79 over-'n-under configuration, and went quietly up the hill.

24 HELL'S LAST DITCH

Mike Talifero had been pacing about the dining room, a pistol in each hand, since the first sounds of battle rent the night.

Two of his lieutenants and an edgy palace guard had stood by their posts at the windows and kept him informed on the developments that were discernible from their observation points.

"Can't see the cars, sir, but I guess he got 'em for sure. Flames are shooting up from down below, near the road I guess."

"Flare back here, sir! High one. 'Bout a hundred yards out."

And the asides:

"How's he hitting both sides at once?"

"Guess it's easy if you know how."

"Everything that bastard does is easy!"

"He just makes it look that way. Try it yourself once."

Then a Talifero bawl: "Shut up! You boys shut up! Look alive there!"

"Christ, sir . . ."

And a heavy *ba-looom* as something hit the roof, shaking the entire structure.

"What the hell was that? What was that?"

"You boys stay put! I'll shoot the first man to run!"

"Christ, sir, he's gonna burn it down!"

A lieutenant yelled, "Isn't anyone shooting back? What the hell are all those boys doing out there?"

"What d'ya shoot back *at*, sir? You can't shoot back at an *explosion!*"

As though to punctuate that remark, the glass-fronted entranceway disappeared with a roar. Flames huffed inside, carrying with them acrid smoke and a million flying slivers of shredded glass.

The lieutenant who had just complained reeled away from that with his face spurting blood like a shower head, clawing at his eyes and groaning. One of the other men grabbed him and steered him to a chair, while Mike Talifero watched with rounded eyes and an entirely sober face.

From outside he could hear one of his men shouting at deserters, and he knew that the tide had turned before the battle was even enjoined.

"Turn some tables over!" he yelled suddenly. "Stack them up at least three deep, and take cover! He'll be coming in! Get ready! Andy! Set up a cross-fire to bracket the doorway! Two of you boys get over there and barricade the side door! *You*, what's your name, and *you!* Just barricade it and stand there! Go through it, and I'll chase you all the way to hell! Understand?"

The free-lancers understood.

Mike Talifero just wished that *he* did.

Just a few hours ago, *twelve fucking hours ago,* the guy had been as good as dead—grounded, hurting, just waiting for them to track him down and snuff him out.

And now, look.

Just look at this!

He could hear engines firing up in the parking lot, could sense their fleeing movements into the night.

How did you handle a thing like . . . ?

He withdrew a small manila envelope from his pocket, shook the little metal emblem out of there, and held it in his palm. Then he spat on it and threw it to the floor.

"Come on, baby," he said half-aloud. "Come on, come on. This is where it's at. Come on and *find* it!"

Bolan came up over the hill with an HE round in the breech of the M-79 and a belt load of alternates slung over his shoulder, including double-aught buckshot, flares, tear gas, and several more rounds of the high explosive powerhouse.

The M-16 riding atop that one-man light-artillery section handled thirty-round clips of 5.56mm. tumblers, deliverable at seven hundred rounds per minute.

A guy came running around the corner from the stables area, a Thompson cradled across his chest, and skidded about two feet into that confrontation with striding death.

Bolan swung the over-'n-under that way and gave the guy one second's worth of the M-16, and that target quit skidding and fell away zipped from groin to throat.

A group of five more who'd been right on his heels promptly tossed Thompsons and shotguns into a pile on the ground and showed the impressive

162

figure in black how high their hands could stretch toward heaven.

He told them in words dropped from an icicle, "Okay, down the hill. Don't pause, and don't look back. Move it!"

They moved it, with vigor, and Bolan went on swiftly across the driveway circle. Some clown poked a light machine gun over the edge of the roof and began spraying slugs wildly into the ground across his route of advance.

Without breaking stride, Bolan angled his multi-weapon upward and squeezed into the pistol grip of the M-79.

A forty-millimeter HE round whizzed into that parapet with a thunderous impact and sent man, gun, and goodly portions of roof tumbling onto the portico.

He coolly inserted another round of high explosives into the slide breech and went on, beneath the portico and inexorably toward that shattered entranceway.

Now it was the Executioner who was smelling blood, and already he was sickening on the overdose.

But it was that kind of world, this Mafia jungle; better their blood than the altar sacrifices of goats both scaped and bled.

Mike Talifero was about four heartbeats removed from the judgment of the universe.

It was no time for the instrument of execution to falter.

He moved on up, kicked aside the twisted aluminum remains of the door casing, and went back into hell.

And it was almost pitiful, this climactic end to the great fox chase of central Jersey.

He was met by two batteries of stacked and over-turned tables, one to either side of the doorway, with nary head nor weapon showing at any edge.

This hardsite had gone mighty soft mighty fast.

A scramble at the far side, accompanied by the angry swearing of Mike SuchIron somewhere in the murky interior, signaled the frantic departure of more battlefield deserters.

The place was filled with smoke, and a lot of heat was coming down from the ceiling area, but he could see a dude in the background, slumped over a table and covering it with blood.

Talifero gave away his position in the rear with an emotional scream, "Open fire! Shoot, shoot, damnit!"

The snout of a Thompson came hesitantly around the side of one of the table-turrets.

Bolan flipped a grenade into that one and dis-patched forty millimeters from the M-79 into the other one.

Tables splintered and flew and rolled all over that place while men in both sectors screamed until Bolan's M-16 mop-up put an end to that agony.

Mike Talifero was yelling something in a strange tongue, and Bolan could dimly see him moving around back there in the smoke—coughing and stumbling about.

Then a door back there opened and closed, and the target of the night abruptly disappeared.

It just had to be.

Bolan knew precisely which door.

The maze had a way of turning back, folding in,

devouring those who played cruel games in her chambers.

He went on, slid in another round of HE, and let it fly into that door, then followed quickly with his own imposing figure.

It was the men's locker room, yeah.

He went in under the cover of his own smoke while selecting another round for the M-79, and he stalked the fox to his final burrow.

And the guy was standing there, in the only place left—in the corner of that shower with Bruno's blood darkly caked about his feet.

Those eyes were positively wild, and there was not a hint of a smile upon the face that had snickered at human agony lo these many years.

He had a gun in each hand, and certainly at least a fighting chance, unlike any he'd ever offered another poor bastard who screamed and pleaded only for death.

But he was frozen there—tongue-tied for probably the first time in his life—stammering something about strong men who die together; but there was nothing truly strong about this man about to die, nothing commendable or admirable.

He was just another cornered punk, alone and contemplating his own death and seeing nothing of value beyond.

Without a word, and from about six paces out, the Executioner squeezed the pistol grip of the M-79 to send a chewing pattern of double-aughts grinding in at chin level.

The pistols clattered to the floor, the body sagged in a flowing river from the shoulders, and a shredded head bounced off the back wall and rolled along the incline toward the drain.

"May his soul thank mine," the Executioner muttered.

He threw a marksman's medal into the gore; then he turned his back on that and walked away from there.

And it was a very short step out of hell.

EPILOGUE

He appropriated one of the few remaining vehicles at Boots and Bugle—ironically enough, a camper van—and calmly withdrew along that trail of tears, taking with him along those darkened Jersey roads new fodder for future nightmares along the river of blood, as well as some fond memories of tender moments agreeably spent.

He heard but did not see the approach of the federal task force screaming into that grim ex-encampment back there in the smoldering ashes of the night, and he mentally tipped his hat to Leo Turrin and Hal Brognola, a couple of true friends who, he was sure, would forever figure in his future —no matter how many lifetimes lay ahead.

He was leaving Jersey with himself in better shape than when he entered. All things considered, that should say something for the place. So he sent a quiet "thank-you" into that corner of quivering universal mold and apologized for all feelings harshly held—while at the same moment promising to return one day for a closer look at the nature of things there.

And when he arrived at the little airstrip "a few miles south" of the hardsite, he was already relaxing into that postcombative torpor and mellowness that characterize a hard campaign honorably met.

Waiting there at that quiet edge of the hell grounds was a sleek executive jet, of the type used by corporations to fly their executives around with style and efficiency. Another type of corporation and a decidedly different sort of executive had been calling the shots for this particular air vehicle; Bolan could think of no more fitting exit for himself from the late and not so great shadow of the Jersey guns.

A single "sentry" waited there, a Marinello hardman with more sand in his eyes than brains in his head; the guy's eyes flickered but briefly into an awakening one startled heartbeat ahead of the flying fist that sent him back into a deeper and perhaps a more peaceful sleep.

The pilot was lying in the aisleway of the cabin, fully dressed, a pillow propped beneath his head, feet crossed, sleeping like a baby.

The Executioner intruded into his dreams and brought him back to the hard world with an awesome black Beretta tickling the tip of his nose.

The guy's eyes flared into an awareness of that which was and must be, and his greeting to the man in black was a quiet, "Oh, hell."

"Let's fly," Bolan suggested, with ice cubes enclosing the words. "Like the birdies. South."

It was to be the sole exchange of dialogue until they reached the southern-flow altitude corridor for air traffic; then the pilot advised Bolan, "You'll have to give me a destination for an ATC clearance."

The man in the co-pilot seat replied, "Forget ATC. Just fly south. I'll tell you when and where to do different."

The pilot showed him a halfhearted smile and agreed, "It's a good night. I can fly visual."

Yes, it was a fairly good night. It had been good to Mack Bolan. And all but a few festering wounds had been expiated into that night.

He shrugged out of his combat rig and tossed it to the rear, then asked the pilot, "You know a fat ghoul they call Sal?"

"No, I—"

"A turkey doctor."

"Oh, hell no. I just fly these people, I don't—"

"When you get home, you pass the word. In the right places. There's a contract on Sal written deep into my guts. You pass that word. Sal is out of business. Or he'd better be."

"Sure, I . . . I'll see that the word gets around."

Bolan sighed, lowered his lids about halfway down those blood-wracked eyes, and settled into a light "combat sleep"—that divided state of consciousness which gave him rest yet kept him animally alert to the outside world.

The pilot was telling him, "Between you and me, Mr. Bolan . . . I mean, just between the two of us, I think you're an okay guy."

The animal side of the Executioner grinned.

Sure.

Sara was okay.

Bruno was okay.

And—for the moment, at least—that wild and woolly universe of Mack Bolan's was okay.

His soul stretched, seeking a shortcut through the maze, sending a gentle probe into that receding countryside down there, giving form to the thought:

Good-bye, Mother Sara. Stay hard.